NAVIGATION AÉRIENNE

LOUIS c.e. GODARD
34, Rue Lavroix, 34.
BATIGNOLLES-PARIS

AÉRONAUTE
du Grand Ballon captif de Paris, 1878-1879
de Nice, 1884. de Turin, 1884

*A L'ÉCOLE AÉROSTATIQUE MILITAIRE ITALIENNE

EXPÉRIENCES & ASCENSIONS
SCIENTIFIQUES

ÉTUDE & CONSTRUCTION D'AÉROSTATS
en tous genres
POUR INVENTEURS & AÉRONAUTES

BALLON CAPTIF A VAPEUR
& Appareils à gaz, roulant,
POUR LES ARMÉES EN CAMPAGNE

DESCENTE EN PARACHUTE

VÉLOCE AÉRIEN

BREVETÉ

GRANDS ATELIERS SPÉCIAUX
de Construction Aérostatique & d'Expériences
35, Rue de la Fédération (Champ de Mars)
& BUREAUX & CORRESPONDANCE
35, Rue Vintimille, PARIS

A ACIER DE...VES
VILLE de NANTES

MAIRIE de NANTES
1 AOUT 87
Bureau des bas-peuld
N° 46½

Paris, le   188

Monsieur le Maire,

J'ai l'honneur de solliciter de votre bienveillance
la faveur de participer à l'éclat des Fêtes de votre
ville.

Je suis muni d'un matériel aérostatique complet,
construit dans mes ateliers et comprenant des Ballons
depuis 300 mètres jusqu'à 2800 mètres cubes, pouvant
enlever de une à dix personnes.

Je me charge de tout genre d'ascension scienti-
fique et avec voyageurs, d'ascension double entre deux
Ballons, de descente en parachute, etc., etc.

Dans l'espoir, Monsieur, que vous voudrez
bien me comprendre dans le Programme de vos Fêtes.

Je vous prie d'agréer l'expression de mes
sentiments distingués.

Louis Godard.

DONA-CEYLON

FINEST

ESTABLISHED IN EDINBURGH SINCE 1869

A UNIQUE INVIGORATING BLEND
of Hearty Black Ceylon Teas

ESTABLISHED IN EDINBURGH SINCE 1869

LEBLANC CADENAS ANTIVOL

LEBLANC CADENAS ANTIVOL

EN ACIER
INDESTRUCTIBLE
INVIOLABLE!

Acierie M. Leblanc — ROUEN

LE TERREUR DE TOUS VOLEURS!

1900   Travaux
1880

FANNY GODARD

E. POTTIER
PHOTOGRAPHE
Maison Julienne
PRÈS LA CATHÉDRALE
ST MALO

THE
DARK LADY
THE WORLD-FAMOUS PRESTIGIOUS BRAND

54 QUALITY CARDS' DECK

GENTLEMEN'S CAPS and HATS
1805   1868
MCARDLE & WILLIAMSON
EXQUISITELY TAILORED FROM THE BEST HIGHLANDS WOOLENS

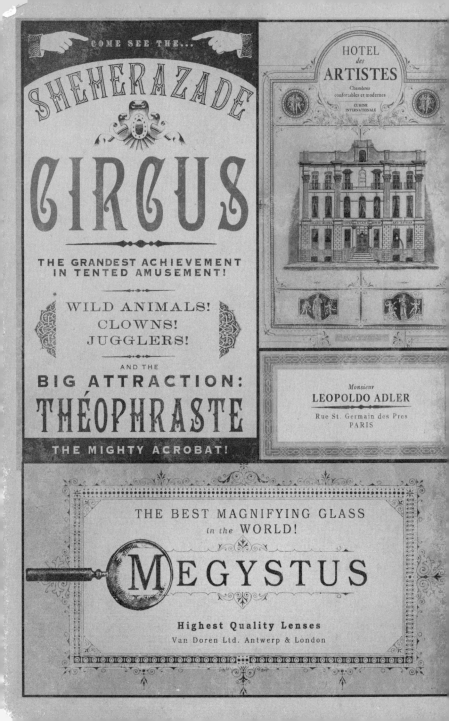

COME SEE THE...

SHEHERAZADE

CIRCUS

THE GRANDEST ACHIEVEMENT IN TENTED AMUSEMENT!

WILD ANIMALS!
CLOWNS!
JUGGLERS!

AND THE

BIG ATTRACTION:
THÉOPHRASTE

THE MIGHTY ACROBAT!

HOTEL
des
ARTISTES

Chambres
confortables et modernes
CUISINE
INTERNATIONALE

Monsieur
LEOPOLDO ADLER

Rue St. Germain des Pres
PARIS

THE BEST MAGNIFYING GLASS
in the WORLD!

MEGYSTUS

Highest Quality Lenses
Van Doren Ltd. Antwerp & London

Sherlock, Lupin & Me is published by Stone Arch Books
A Capstone Imprint
1710 Roe Crest Drive
North Mankato, Minnesota 56003
www.capstonepub.com

All names, characters and related indicia contained in this book, copyright of Atlantyca
Dreamfarm s.r.l., are exclusively licensed to Atlantyca S.p.A. in their original version. Their
translated and/or adapted versions are property of Atlantyca S.p.A. All rights reserved.

© 2011 Atlantyca Dreamfarm s.r.l., Italy
© 2014 for this book in English language - (Stone Arch Books)
Text by Pierdomenico Baccalario and Alessandro Gatti
Translated by Chris Turner
Original edition published by Edizioni Piemme S.p.A., Italy
Original title: Il trio della Dama Nera

International Rights © Atlantyca S.p.A., via Leopardi 8 - 20123 Milano – Italia -
foreignrights@atlantyca.it- www.atlantyca.com
No part of this book may be stored, reproduced or transmitted in any form or by any
means, electronic or mechanical, including photocopying, recording, or by any information
storage and retrieval system, without written permission from the copyright holder. For
information address Atlantyca S.p.A.

Cataloging-in-Publication Data is available at the Library of Congress website.
ISBN: 978-1-4342-6523-4 (library binding)
ISBN: 978-1-4342-6526-5 (paperback)
ISBN: 978-1-62370-040-9 (paper-over-board)

Summary: While on summer vacation, little Irene Adler meets a young William Sherlock
Holmes. The two share stories of pirates and have battles of wit while running wild on
the sunny streets and rooftops. When Sherlock's friend, Lupin, joins in on the fun, they all
become fast friends. But the good times end abruptly when a dead body floats ashore on
the nearby beach. The young detective trio will have to put all three of their heads together
to solve this mystery.

Designer: Veronica Scott

Printed in China by Nordica.
0514/CA21400802
052014   008217R

IRENE ADLER

SHERLOCK LUPIN & ME

THE DARK LADY

by *Irene Adler*

Illustrations by Jacopo Bruno

STONE ARCH BOOKS™

TABLE OF CONTENTS

Chapter 1

THREE FRIENDS

Would you believe that I was the first and only girlfriend of Sherlock Holmes, the famous detective? When we met, though, he wasn't a detective yet. And he wasn't famous. I was twelve, and he was only a little older than me.

It was summer — the sixth of July, to be exact. And I can still remember perfectly the time I first met him. He was sitting in a corner on top of the city walls, his back up against the creeping ivy. In the sky above him, seagulls circled in slow spirals. There was nothing beyond him but the sea — an endless expanse of dark and sparkling blue. Sherlock had his chin resting on his knees and he was completely absorbed in reading a book. He was almost scowling at it, as if the world depended on him finishing it.

I don't think he would have even noticed me if I hadn't spoken to him. Since I'd just come to Saint-Malo, I asked him if he lived here. "No," he said without even taking his eyes off his book. "I live in a house. Forty-nine Rue Saint Sauveur."

What a strange sense of humor, I thought. Of course he didn't live on top of a wall by the sea! I knew that a battle of wits had just begun between us.

I wasn't from the city of Saint-Malo. I'd only just arrived after a long carriage ride from Paris. We were on vacation, and staying there had been my mother's idea. I was excited. Until then, I'd only seen the sea a few times when I'd gone with Papa to Calais, where he took the ship to England. I'd seen it once in Sanremo in Italy, too, but my parents said I was too young to remember that. But I did remember it. I really did. So the idea of spending all of the summer of 1870 at a seaside resort was wonderful. And my father had even said that we could stay longer if we wanted to. So, even though I eventually had to go back to school, this was going to be a nice and long summer. And it turned out to be the summer that changed my whole life.

The trip to Saint-Malo had been terrible. The problem wasn't the carriage, which my father had spent a lot of money to hire (as he always did when he was looking after my mother and me). It was a carriage fit for a king, with four black horses, a coachman with a top hat, and seats covered with silk cushions. Even still, the six-hour trip under the watchful gaze of Mama and Mr. Nelson made it seem like an eternity.

Mr. Horatio Nelson was our butler. He was very tall, very quiet, and seemed very concerned about every little thing I did. The rest of the servants had left the week before to prepare our summer house for us. Mr. Nelson was the only one who'd stayed back. And he never took his eyes off me. He always seemed to be about to say to me, "Perhaps it is not appropriate for a lady to behave that way, Miss Irene."

Perhaps it is not appropriate, Miss Irene, I thought. Mr. Nelson always said that whenever I was doing anything fun. And that was probably why, at the first chance I got, I escaped from our summer house and climbed up the winding path to the top of the city walls.

Our vacation home had two floors. Although it was small, it was very pretty, with a big skylight in the roof and bigger bow windows (which I used to call "boat windows" when I was little). There was a trellis covered in ivy that crept all over the walls. When we first got there, my mother said, "Heavens! That ivy will be just full of animals!"

It took a few days before I realized what she'd meant. I'd left my bedroom window open one night, and the next morning Mr. Nelson found a snake slithering across the floor! "Perhaps it is not appropriate, Miss Irene, to leave the window open at night," Mr. Nelson had said sternly, entering my room. He'd then taken the poker from the fireplace and began to walk toward the snake.

"Please don't kill it, Mr. Nelson!" I'd cried.

Mr. Nelson then sighed, put the poker down, and grabbed the snake in his hands. "Then I shall politely escort our little guest to the garden." Mr. Nelson was a grumpy man, but he always knew how to make me laugh.

As soon as he'd left the room with my so-called guest, the wardrobe door popped open and a boy with a skinny face popped out. He was my other great friend during that long summer. His name was Arsène Lupin, the famous gentleman thief. But back then he hadn't yet begun his dazzling criminal career. And he was hardly a gentleman, considering he was only a couple of years older than I was, and even younger than Sherlock Holmes.

Now you know the names of my friends. If you've guessed that a lot happened that summer, you'd be right. But it's best if I start at the beginning . . .

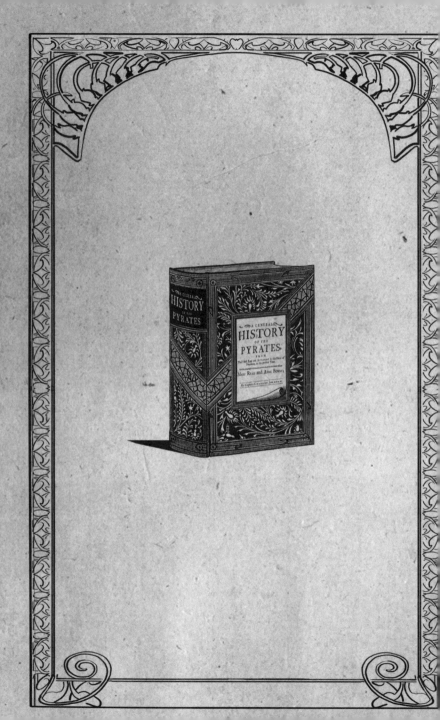

Chapter 2

THE ART OF ESCAPE

After we arrived at our summer home, Mother was busy helping the servants unpack our trunks and suitcases. There was no way I was going to waste an afternoon doing that! So I escaped by the small gate at the back of the garden. From there, I found the winding alleyways of the town, the promontory, and then the walls. The first person I'd come across was the bookish boy I mentioned earlier. I didn't know anything about him except that he was very rude and spoke English.

I put my hands on my hips and tilted my head

slightly, just like my mother did when she was trying to attract my father's attention. "Hello," I said.

But Sherlock Holmes didn't seem even a little bit interested in giving me any of his attention. So I tried another approach. "What are you reading?" I asked.

"A book," he said flatly.

"And you're still on the first page?" I asked.

At least my joke annoyed him a little. He stuck a finger in the book to keep his place and looked up at me, his eyes blazing. "Have you ever heard of René Duguay-Trouin?" he asked.

"No," I said.

"Ha!" he said. "Then your skills of observation are very poor." Having said that, he stuck his nose back into his book. Normally I would have tossed some smart remark back at him, but that day I didn't care to. I was too happy about having the whole summer ahead of me in that beautiful seaside town to bicker with the first person I'd met.

I went over to the parapet and looked down. A strip of white sand stretched out in a jagged line in front of me. I gazed across at the little harbor, the promontory, and the two tiny islands that were no more than a hundred yards from the shore. Only then did I notice the statue of a man on top of a pedestal just a few feet from us.

"That's René Duguay-Trouin," whispered Sherlock, pointing at the statue.

I jumped up onto the parapet and sat down to inspect the statue. "He was a hero of the high seas!" I said. I could hear the waves behind me. The feeling of empty space from the top of those high ramparts made me feel giddy.

"He was a pirate," Sherlock said, correcting me. He turned a couple of pages then continued speaking. "He was born here in 1673, the eighth of ten children. Five of them died almost as soon as they were born."

"He didn't die, though."

"No," Sherlock said. "He went to sea and became one of the most famous pirates of his time."

I let my legs dangle in the air, pretending I wasn't listening. He stopped talking and pretended to read. A few minutes went by. But then I caught him looking at me from behind his book. I started laughing.

"What's wrong with you?" he said.

"I'm laughing because you were looking at me," I said.

"No I wasn't," Sherlock said.

"Yes you were. You were peeking out at me from behind your book!"

Sherlock grunted, and then moved around, trying to find a more comfortable position in his ivy-covered spot.

I couldn't help but chuckle as I looked at the statue of the man in his hat with a sword in one hand. I thought about all the useless information the boy had just told me about him. Pirates, swords, blah, blah, blah. Boys always talk about boring, meaningless stuff.

"Anyway, my name's Irene," I said cheerfully. "How about you? Do you have a name?"

"I have two, actually — William Sherlock," he said in a mocking tone. "But everyone calls me William."

"That's probably because Sherlock sounds a little odd!" I said. He thought long and hard instead of responding. After a few moments, I finally said, "Well, I think they're wrong. William is very boring. Sherlock suits you better."

"If you say so . . ." he said.

"Absolutely!" I said. "In fact, I've decided that from now on I'm going to call you Sherlock!"

He shrugged. "If you like. It's only a name."

"Have you and your brother lived in Saint-Malo a long time?" I asked.

He raised an eyebrow at me but said nothing.

I smiled. "You said that my skills of observation were very poor earlier," I said, pointing to the statue. "Maybe you're right. But I do know that you're not French, because we're talking in English and your accent is too good for you to have learned it at school. Also, you're not dressed like someone on vacation at the seaside, which probably means you live here. You have a sour expression on your face, like someone who's just argued with someone or run away from home — like me. And when you told me that five of the pirate's brothers had died, your eyes lit up, so I deduced that you've just had a fight with your own brother." I took a deep breath. "So, how close did I get?"

Sherlock's eyes were full of honest surprise, an expression that was very different from the cold but brilliant sneer that everyone came to know him by many years later when he grew up to be the greatest detective in the world. He closed his book. I smiled to myself. Apparently, I'd finally gotten his attention.

"You speak English but you're not English," he said.

"I'm American," I said, ruining the guessing game.

"But you live in Paris."

"Yes, I do." But I wondered how he'd figured that out. I was wearing a dress, shoes, and white socks. There was nothing particularly Parisian about my appearance. "Is it that obvious?"

Sherlock chuckled. "Not at all. It was nothing but a guess. But you're not wearing the right shoes for the beach or walking in the countryside. So you've probably just arrived. You said that you've just run away from home, so I assume you're not just passing through. But you don't look scared, like someone who's running away from something they're frightened of. So, you must have run away for some other reason. You're probably here on vacation with your parents." His voice was calm and reassuring. Almost musical. Our little game continued.

"And do I have any sisters?" I asked.

Sherlock thought for a moment, then shook his head. "No."

"Brothers?" I asked.

"I've been thinking about that," Sherlock said. "From the way you spoke to me, I'd say so. An older brother, probably."

"Wrong, Sherlock!" I said.

"You're an only child, then," he said.

"Yes," I said, swinging my legs. "You're very good. You almost guessed everything, except for my parents, since only my mother is here."

"I'm so sorry for your loss," Sherlock said quickly. "I didn't mean to —"

"Hold your horses!" I said. "My father's fine. It's just that he didn't come on vacation with us because he had to work. He works with trains and railways. But he was the one who chose this place. The three of us came here today: me, my mother, and Mr. Nelson." I noticed the shadow that passed over Sherlock's face when I was talking about my father. I didn't realize it then, but his father had died eight years earlier.

"What are you reading?" I asked.

He checked the cover as if he'd forgotten. "*A General History of the Pyrates,* by Captain Charles Johnson."

"Is it interesting?"

"Oh, yes," he said. "Very."

"And you'd like to be one?" I asked.

"Like to be one what?"

"A pirate."

Sherlock chuckled before answering, "Quite frankly, it had never occurred to me."

"I'd like to be one," I said. "And I'd be a good pirate. Or is that piratess?"

"I don't think there's such a word as piratess," he said. "There haven't been enough female pirates."

"That's too bad," I said. "I'd be an excellent pirate! I'd give orders to everyone and have an island all to myself. Batten down the hatches! Hoist that mizzen! Ahoy, me hearties!"

Sherlock smirked. Then I heard Mr. Nelson calling my name. He was some way off and his voice echoed from down among the alleyways. He kept repeating it. "Miss Adler! Miss Adler!" he called.

How embarrassing! I thought. *What a delightful way to be introduced to someone new.*

My new friend was looking at me, studying my reactions. I jumped down off the wall, looked at the harbor, the sea, and one of the little islands near the promontory. For a second I imagined it was a treasure island, complete with a galleon with a Jolly Roger waving in the wind. "I have to escape, Sherlock," I said. "Mr. Nelson, our butler, will be here soon."

"Escape?"

"You heard me," I said. "I don't want him to take me back home."

"He sounds worried," Sherlock said.

"He isn't. My mother must have sent him. Whether I go home with him now or go home later in time for dinner, I'm going to get scolded. So I might as well make it worth the trouble."

"I understand," Sherlock said.

I went over to some stone stairs that led down to the beach and pretended to plan my escape down the stairs. "I'm not going to spend the rest of the day putting linen and clothes into closets," I said. "Or, even worse, playing card games."

"How horrid," Sherlock said. I didn't know if he meant the clothes or the cards. It was all a game, though. I knew full well that the servants would put away all the linen, and my mother hardly ever played cards. But Sherlock couldn't have known that.

"Miss Adler!" Mr. Nelson called, closer now.

I put my hands on my hips again. "So, Sherlock? Are you going to sit there and read your book, or are you going to help me escape?"

Sherlock thought for a moment. He shut his book about pirates and put it in a small cloth bag. "This way," he said. He walked over to a path that was so narrow it was little more than a crack between the rocks. He led me down. Our hands accidentally brushed and he immediately pulled away as if he'd been burned. He turned his back to me and we walked quickly and without talking for what seemed a very long time.

When we got to the bottom of the walls, we began to follow them toward the harbor. "Where are we going?" I asked softly.

"To a friend's place," Sherlock said. Seeing him on his feet made me realize he was tall and very thin. His cotton jacket flicked against his protruding ribs as he moved. Every time he stopped, he'd hunch over and kind of fold in on himself, as if he were trying to hide. But as soon as he started walking again, his back would straighten completely.

"And who's this friend?" I asked.

"He's got a rowboat," Sherlock said. "A very small one. Well, it's not his rowboat, it's his father's."

"And you want to go out to sea in it?" I asked.

"That's generally the function of boats," he said with a grin.

I couldn't believe it. I'd just arrived in Saint-Malo and already I'd met a boy. Not only that, the boy was about to take me out on a boat. "That's . . . wonderful!" I cried.

And that's how Sherlock Holmes took me to the harbor to meet his friend with a boat — and the time when all our troubles first began.

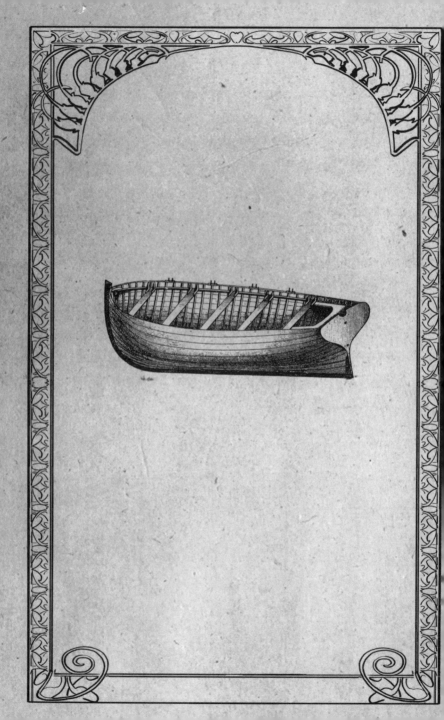

Chapter 3

ASHCROFT MANOR

Sherlock's friend turned out to be a skinny but strong-looking boy. His eyes and hair were as dark as Sherlock's. He was busy cleaning out the bottom of a rowboat that was tied to the end of the pier.

I wiped my brow. The sun was scorching hot. Seagulls were perched up on the masts of the boats, while fishermen were mending their nets. I only had eyes for the boats as they bobbed on the water, promising me relief and relaxation.

"Apparently there's an emergency, Lupin," Sherlock said as soon as we reached the boat.

"What kind of emer —" the boy began, but he

went silent the second he saw me. He froze as still as a statue.

"This is Irene," Sherlock said.

"Hello," I said.

"Hello," the other boy said.

"And this is Lupin," Sherlock said.

"Lupin?" I repeated, puzzled. "That's a strange name."

"My friend isn't as clever as I am when it comes to names," Sherlock said with a grin.

"My real name's Arsène," the boy said. "But I prefer to be called Lupin."

"Are you French?" I asked.

He nodded. "And what about you?" he asked. "What's your story?"

"She's running away from home," Sherlock butted in, hunched over his skinny, knobbly legs. "Nothing serious, though," he added. "But you know how it is with parents."

"She'd just prefer to get away from her family for a while," Lupin suggested.

"Exactly," I said.

"Did you get in a fight with your sister?"

I shook my head.

"Your mother?"

"Horatio Nelson," I said. "But we didn't fight. It's just I don't want to go home at the moment."

"Irene's on vacation," Sherlock explained. "And I told her I had a friend who doesn't ask a lot of questions."

The two boys exchanged a look that seemed to mean, "We need to talk."

Lupin put down his bucket and pointed to the rope that held the boat to the pier. "No problem," he said. "Untie that knot and jump on board. Do you have a swimsuit?"

"No," I said, scowling for some reason.

"Well, then just be careful you don't fall in," Lupin said.

The boat was tossed about by the waves. It really was tiny, with only two places to sit: one at the oars, and one a little farther forward.

At the back of the boat there was a pile of ropes, fishing nets, and assorted items Lupin had collected when he went diving. The two of them made me sit at the front while they squeezed in between the oars, taking one oar each. Like two old sea dogs, they rowed in perfect time with each other, and the boat glided gently out from the harbor.

"So, who's this Horatio Nelson?" Lupin eventually asked me. "And how come he's got the same name as a British admiral?"

I didn't know exactly, so I didn't answer right away. Mr. Horatio Nelson had always just been Mr. Horatio Nelson to me. I'd never asked myself why. He'd always worked for my mother's family, even after the War for Southern Independence.

I looked at the harbor behind us as we slowly moved out to sea. The boat tilted up with every stroke and then dipped back down into the water. There were a lot of other boats all around us, all of them much larger and more impressive than ours. It felt a little like being a minnow.

We were just rounding the promontory when I heard a shout from the shore and saw some startled gulls fly away. I smiled. "Maybe you can ask him in person," I said, pointing at the street. Mr. Nelson was standing there, waving at me and calling, trying to get my attention.

"Miss Adler! Miss Adler!" he cried. "Where are you going?"

My two friends instantly stopped rowing, appearing to be as frightened as if my mother's huge butler had been in the boat along with us. I signaled to them to keep rowing. "Don't be afraid. He won't do anything to you."

I waved to Mr. Nelson, trying to make him understand that I was fine and that he didn't need to worry about me. "I'll be back soon!" I yelled, waving a white handkerchief. "Everything's all right!"

"Let's hope so," Lupin whispered, giving the worried butler a long look. "He's very big and very angry."

"It doesn't matter," I said, continuing to wave to Mr. Nelson, who was now running along the beach trying to keep up. "I'm pretty sure he doesn't know how to swim!"

"And if you're wrong?" my new friends both asked together.

I shrugged and grinned. They continued to dip the oars into the calm water of the Atlantic, a little faster now.

After we'd rounded the promontory, Mr. Nelson gave up the chase. He stood there for a while, as still as a statue, with one foot up on a rock and the sun shining off his head. Then he turned and went back the way he came.

We rowed between the two islands that I'd seen from up on the walls. Sherlock and Lupin told me that when the tide went out, you could reach them via a stone walkway that was now just below the surface of the sea.

"I just hope he doesn't think we've kidnapped you," Lupin repeated several times. "You wanted to run away?"

I shrugged. "Yes, but don't worry. When I get home, I'll just get the usual lecture from my mother."

"The usual?" Sherlock asked, raising an eyebrow.

"This isn't the first time I've wanted a little freedom!" I said, then laughed. "What's so weird about that?"

"Well, it's not really normal for a girl to get in trouble a lot," he said.

"I've always been like this," I said, feeling my chest tighten. "I'm used to getting scolded."

I looked around. We were past the first island and were now rounding the second. Almost hidden among the bushes was a building. I pointed it out to my new friends. "What's that?" I asked.

"A fort," answered Lupin. "There's nothing there but a French flag flapping in the wind."

The boys rowed on. The sun was scorching, so I put a hand in the water to enjoy its coolness flowing over me. I looked at the handful of houses built among the trees and rocks, and the even fewer people on the beach. Back then, it wasn't popular to go the beach. Gentlemen preferred ladies with pale, white skin.

As I scanned the jagged coastline I asked, "Where are we going?"

"To Ashcroft Manor," said Lupin.

"Are the Ashcrofts friends of yours?" I asked.

He shook his head and pointed with his chin. "It's an old, deserted mansion, right at the end of the beach. The road there is covered in brambles. They say that the only thing that's there now is the ghost of old man Ashcroft."

"Which is utter nonsense," Sherlock said sharply.

I smiled. Lupin was obviously trying to weave an air of mystery around Ashcroft Manor. But Sherlock was trying just as hard to unravel it.

"An old, deserted mansion," I repeated. "Sounds interesting."

"It isn't," Sherlock said tersely. "Empty rooms with dust everywhere. Nothing to see."

Lupin dug his elbow into Sherlock's side. "Don't listen to him," Lupin said. "It's a really cool place. It's kind of become our secret hideout."

"Your secret hideout?" I asked.

"When we want to get away from trouble, we go there," Lupin said.

"And what trouble do you have to get away from?" I asked, full of curiosity.

Lupin didn't answer right away. While I was waiting for him to speak, I started to think that Sherlock and Lupin looked like brothers, even though they weren't. They exchanged glances like they were trying to work out which secrets to share and which ones to keep to themselves. And there did seem to be something incredibly interesting about what they wanted to hide from me. I wanted to understand what they were saying with their eyes and wanted to know the reason they weren't telling me things. I felt like a thief struggling with a complicated lock to some treasure chest.

"Well, you know, trouble," mumbled Lupin. "But it's not like we get into really bad trouble."

"Just the usual," Sherlock added.

"Such as?" I asked.

"His brother and sister, for instance," Lupin said.

"You have a brother and sister?" I asked Sherlock.

He nodded with a sideways smile. "An older brother and a younger sister. And both of them make me wish I were an only child."

"How about you?" I asked Lupin.

"I am an only child," he said. He threw his hands in the air, letting go of his oar and then grabbing it again with the speed of a magician. "But my family is crazy."

Sherlock chuckled. "You can say that again."

"So, when you can't take it anymore," I said, "you take the boat out here?"

"That's right," said Lupin.

The thought of two strong boys escaping to their

secret mansion together made me chuckle. "And when you're there," I asked, "what do you do?"

"Well, for starters there are lots of rooms to explore," said Lupin. "Old Ashcroft's study, the cellar, and the attic . . ."

"That's right, there are lots of rooms. And all of them empty." Sherlock said wryly, earning himself another elbow in the ribs from his friend. "I admit, it's not the most exciting place in the world."

"So, why do you go there if it's so boring?" I asked Sherlock.

Sherlock grinned. "It's one of the only places I can read in peace," he said.

I looked at Sherlock's long, thin arms as he rowed. Lupin's arms were bigger and had smooth muscles. Sherlock's skin was pale, while Lupin had a farmer's suntan. When Sherlock moved, he looked rigid, as if he didn't have any joints to his bones. But when Lupin moved, he looked like a nimble wildcat. It was hard to imagine two more different-looking boys.

At the end of a sweeping curve of the island, the beach was swallowed up by lush vegetation. The roof of an old house suddenly emerged at the end of the strip of land, surrounded by low trees, grass, and boulders.

"Welcome to Ashcroft Manor," Sherlock mumbled, lifting his oar.

Chapter 4

DO YOU PLAY?

The old mansion stood back from the beach on top of a rocky slope. It was made of wood, with a flat black roof and huge windows that overlooked the sea. On the beach next to the manor were round boulders that looked like huge toys a giant had left behind.

We pulled the boat up onto the beach near a narrow path that led to the house across a jungle of weeds that used to be a front lawn.

Once we got closer, I could see how rundown the mansion really was. Overgrown plants and trees looked like they were attacking the house from behind. There was a veranda overlooking the sea, but it was piled high with pieces of broken furniture and assorted junk. The shutters on the top floor were nailed closed, and the roof was damaged in several spots. The paint was peeling off the walls.

It was all a terrible shame, seeing what would have been a beautiful house in such disarray. But there was also something vaguely disturbing about the mansion. It was bathed in sunlight and just a stone's throw from the sea, but it somehow seemed wrapped in a gray cloud that it had created all by itself, like a shadow that seeped out from the inside.

No one said anything, but none of us moved to go inside. We sat on the shell-encrusted rocks and watched the sea and the coastline, which trailed away toward the promontory and the two islands.

"Where's your house?" Lupin eventually asked.

I gestured vaguely toward the pointed roofs of the town. "Over there."

"Yes, but does it have an address?" Lupin asked.

"I don't remember," I said. Then I laughed. I hadn't even thought about it when I opened the gate at the back of the garden. "Actually, I have no idea where my house is!"

"So, how will you get back?" Sherlock asked.

"I don't think it will be too difficult," I said. "It's a two-level house, like this one, with a small garden, and a gate that opens onto a lane that leads to the town."

"Can you see the sea?" Sherlock asked.

I thought for a while before answering, "Yes."

They both continued asking me questions until, little by little, they were able to figure out where my new summer home was. It was very close to where Sherlock lived. That explained why we'd found ourselves up on the same section of the walls looking for a little peace and quiet.

We talked for a long time that afternoon, as you do when you meet someone new and interesting. Time flies and you end up chatting about everything as if the day has no end. I listened to my new friends and learned a lot about them.

Perhaps in my memories I'm exaggerating the number of things we spoke about that long afternoon. One thing I do remember perfectly clearly, though, is that when we got back into the boat and rowed back to the harbor we were all very tired. I even tried rowing for a while to give Sherlock a break, but we just started going in circles. No one talked. Instead, we just listened to the waves and watched the sun as it sank slowly below the horizon.

We climbed up onto the pier as the evening shadows were growing long. Lupin quickly secured his boat to the pier. Lupin stood for a few seconds in front of me before saying goodbye. He was probably wondering if it would be all right to kiss me on the cheek, like you do with relatives. I can still remember him blushing and then trying to hide his handsome face in the shadows.

"Um . . . see you tomorrow?" he said finally. I nodded and smiled.

Since we'd just discovered we were almost neighbors, Sherlock and I walked home together. He walked a little ahead of me and rather quickly. There was something anxious about his brisk pace, as if he were in a hurry to get home.

"Sherlock? Is everything all right?" I asked him, catching up to him.

He pulled out a watch attached to a belt loop by a silver chain and checked the time. "I've got to get home before my mother comes back from bridge."

"Do you play cards?" I asked.

"Yes," he answered with a sigh. "But I don't particularly like card games. My mother, on the other hand, was playing bridge with her friends before anyone else in town had even heard of the game. They play almost every day. And if when she gets back everything isn't neat and tidy . . ." Sherlock trailed off. He seemed so embarrassed that I realized that he was hiding something else from me: He had to go home because he had to do the cooking for everyone. I pretended I hadn't seen his embarrassment and said something stupid to change the subject. From the smile that appeared on his face, I realized he was grateful.

We walked for about ten minutes, following a low stone wall. Sherlock eventually stopped outside a clean, modest-looking house that was just a few blocks from mine. "Do you know how to get home?" he asked.

I said I did. I recognized a few things along the street. "See you tomorrow, Sherlock."

"See you tomorrow," he said before rushing off.

I thought about my two new friends as I walked home. When I reached the garden gate, I pushed it open. It squeaked loudly.

The second he saw me, Mr. Nelson's baritone voice roared, "Miss Adler!" His whole face seemed to be twitching. His eyes looked like they were about to pop out. "We'd barely arrived! Two strangers — probably thugs, the both of them! The dangerous sea, away for hours and hours . . . You didn't give your mother a second thought! We were all so worried! Where did you go and what were you doing?!"

I didn't even bother to argue as he laid out all the things I'd done wrong — all of them were indisputable and unquestionable. I tossed my hands in the air, surrendering. Then I went to my room without pleading for mercy. But just before I went in, I looked at Mr. Nelson and said, "I'm sorry." Then I closed the door behind me and waited for Mr. Nelson to lock the door from outside like he always did when I got in trouble.

I heard the key turning in the lock. "You will stay in your room until your mother says you can come out," he said.

I went to investigate my bathroom. When I went in, I couldn't help but smile — Mr. Nelson might have locked me in my room, but before he did, he'd brought me up a basin of hot water and clean towels.

"Thank you, Mr. Nelson," I murmured.

I looked in the mirror. I was sunburned and my hair had been tumbled about by the wind. But my eyes were sparkling with happiness.

* * *

Later that evening, as I lay in bed smelling the beautiful dinner they were eating downstairs, the word "strangers" kept reaching my ears. My mother had said it at least a dozen times during dinner as she interrogated Mr. Nelson about my reckless behavior, which had apparently ruined her entire day. She loved to tell anyone who would listen how disobedient, uncontrollable, and immature I was, and today was no exception. Judging by how much she was carrying on and on about all the things I'd done wrong that afternoon, she was likely rehearsing what she'd later present to my father as evidence for punishment when he came to visit.

"Strangers," my mother said again to Mr. Nelson.

She's wrong, I thought. I gazed out my window at the stars in the indigo sky. *Lupin and Sherlock aren't strangers.* It was like we'd been friends forever. As if we were all old friends who'd been reunited after a long, long time apart.

Chapter 5

THE CASTAWAY

The next day, I ran to the front of the Holmes' house. Their garden was neat and tidy. The front door was closed, as were the shutters. There wasn't a soul in sight. *Maybe no one's home,* I thought.

"Sherlock!" I called. "Sherlock? Are you home?" Finally, I heard noise from inside. Someone moved a chair, then something made of glass fell to the floor. Then I heard a muffled curse.

A shutter on the first floor opened. In the dark frame of the window, the rugged face of a young man appeared. He looked to be about twenty. His hair was slicked back, his eyes were round, and he had a blank gaze on his face. "Is it market day?" he grumbled at me. "What have you got for us? Melons? Vegetables? Shellfish? Something else?"

Feeling irritated, I took a step back. I wasn't annoyed because he'd mistaken me for a grocer's girl, but because he was speaking without even bothering to look at me. "I believe you have made a mistake, my Lord," I answered with just the right amount of coldness. "I am a friend of William Sherlock Holmes, Esquire. Is he available, please?"

"A friend!?" exclaimed the young man. "Now there's a surprise. William!" he shouted back into the house. "William! Hurry up!"

Visibly out of breath, Sherlock appeared at the front door. "William!" the young man continued to call. "William! Where have you gone?"

"I'm here!" said my friend, looking at me and then up at the young man in the window. He lifted a hand. "Everything's all right! Get back to your reading. We're going for a ride."

I guessed from the way Sherlock spoke to him that the young man at the window was Sherlock's older brother.

"Aren't you going to introduce me to your girlfriend?" the older boy asked.

"Another time, maybe! See you later!" Sherlock said, hurrying to get away. He gave me a pleading look and pointed to the street that led down to the harbor. Then he immediately changed his mind. "Actually, let's go this way!"

I let him walk his usual three steps ahead of me. As soon as we'd gone around a corner and were out of sight of his brother, I stopped dead in the middle of the street. "Nice to see you, Sherlock!" I said, pretending to be annoyed.

He put his hands up in the air as if I were threatening him with a gun. "I'm sorry!" he cried. "I'm sorry. It's just that I didn't want you to meet, um . . ."

"Your brother?" I offered.

"Yes! We just don't get along," Sherlock stammered. "He's . . ."

"He's handsome," I said with a grin.

Sherlock suddenly put his hands down. "He's what?!"

"I said he's handsome. How old is he? Twenty?" I asked.

"Twenty-one," Sherlock grumbled.

"And what does he do?" I asked.

"Nothing! He does absolutely nothing!" he exclaimed, turning red. "He's the laziest, least ambitious person I've ever met! He's totally incapable of doing anything helpful!"

"He's the opposite of you, then," I said.

"What do you mean?" Sherlock asked.

"If lazy, unambitious people make you this angry, then it means you're different," I said. "You're probably a very practical person."

"Well, I suppose," Sherlock said. "Certainly more than he is."

He began walking again with his inimitable stride, assuming that I was following him. But I didn't move an inch, remaining in the shade of the wall next to me. It took a long time before he realized that he was walking by himself.

He suddenly stopped and turned with a surprised expression on his face. He lifted his eyebrows and asked me, "What are you doing?"

"I'm giving you your first lesson in practicality, my dear Sherlock," I said. "When we see each other, I'd like you to say 'hello.'" I didn't really expect him to smile pleasantly or anything big. I just wanted a simple greeting.

He snorted. "I see!" he said. "And what else would you like?"

"Well, you could also smile pleasantly," I said, teasing him.

Sherlock walked back to me. His cheeks were flushed, but I didn't know if it was because he was laughing, because he was angry, or because he was embarrassed. "What is this nonsense!?"

He was angry. I spoke calmly and quietly in my sweetest voice. "It's called manners, Sherlock. You and I had agreed to meet, hadn't we? Well, here I am. I had to stay in my room all night and didn't get any dinner. I wish I could get something to eat, but we seem to be walking away from the town." I smiled. "Would you like to tell me where we're going or should I just follow you in silence?"

There were a lot of questions for Sherlock to ponder. He opened his mouth, not knowing where to begin. It was obvious that he wasn't used to being spoken to like this.

"You can apologize now," I said. "And then you can take me to get something to eat."

★ ★ ★

At the shop, I was given so much bread, herring, and mustard that I got the impression they'd never seen a silver coin before. Outside the shop, I pulled off a piece of bread, dipped it in the mustard, and ate it so quickly my throat burned for the rest of the day.

After, we walked along the same stretch of beach we'd followed the day before. This time we traveled along a dirt track that snaked its way under a lush, green canopy. "Where are we going?" I asked, even though I'd already figured out the answer.

"Ashcroft Manor," Sherlock said. "Lupin should already be there."

It took us almost half an hour to reach the dilapidated, old house. The last part of the journey was the most difficult. The path bypassed the house and plunged into a distant forest. We had to cross a field overgrown with sun-scorched grass and thorns.

As Sherlock had predicted, Lupin was already there. He just sat with his back to us, staring out to sea. "Hello!" he exclaimed, without turning around.

"Lupin," Sherlock said. He jumped down off the bank and onto one of the boulders on the beach. He stood there for a moment, wondering if he should help me down or just let me take care of myself, as if I were a boy. You know, one of them — not some little girl with pale, scratched legs who insisted on polite smiles and good manners. He chose the middle ground. He stepped off the boulder but stayed close, just in case I needed him. I just jumped down onto the sand without thinking.

"Irene," Lupin said, this time turning around.

When I saw his face, I screamed. Lupin had a bloody scar right across his forehead and he was grinning horribly with ugly, crooked teeth. He looked at Sherlock, turned his palms up questioningly, and asked, "What do you think?"

Sherlock's expression first showed fear, then bewilderment, then laughter. I realized it might be better to stop screaming. I then noticed that there was a strange-looking leather case by Lupin's feet. And that my new friend didn't seem to be in a lot of pain from his injury.

"So?" Lupin said, first looking at Sherlock and then at me. "How does it look?"

"It's fabulous!" answered Sherlock. "It looks real!"

He started touching the scar, but Lupin jumped back. "Hey! You can't touch it!"

Sherlock crossed his arms. "Fine," he said.

I couldn't figure out what was going on. Lupin pretended to fall down, laughed again, and then showed me the same maniacal grin that I'd seen before. "The teeth are amazing, aren't they?"

Lupin put a finger in his mouth, moved his lips up, and, with a dull plop, false teeth dropped out. "Voilà!" he said. "I fooled you, didn't I?!"

Lupin and Sherlock sat cross-legged on the sand next to the leather case. "Would you mind telling me what's going on?" I said, slowly regaining my composure.

"Have I told you what my father does?" Lupin said. "He's an acrobat, a tightrope walker, and a circus performer. And this is his bag of tricks."

I approached cautiously, almost suspiciously. In the case were masks, wigs, weird false teeth, noses, hairpieces, brushes, and cans of glue. There was also an arsenal of fake mustaches, beards, face powder, and lipsticks. "And can we use them?" I asked, fascinated. I dropped my bag of bread, mustard, and herring, not caring that they fell onto the sand.

"Absolutely not!" Lupin said with a grin. He grabbed a wig out of the case. "Who'll go first?"

We spent the whole day dressing up and pretending we were heroes and heroines, reciting the few lines from plays we had committed to memory.

Sherlock was a natural. His face changed completely with a few brush strokes and a mustache, and his voice transformed just as easily. He could play the role of King Lear, Henry V, or a Sicilian soldier.

Lupin was the most elegant in the way he moved, which somehow made him perfect for playing crazy characters. He looked so enthusiastic and dramatic. With a wig and white makeup around his eyes, he could even look like a monkey. With a bandana tied around his perfectly round head, he became a pirate. With a beard, he became a castaway. With a little clay powder and hair cream, he transformed into a desert prince.

As for me, I was so happy playing with the makeup, wigs, and fake jewels that I began to sing as if I was performing in some Italian opera. Sherlock and Lupin were acting out a death scene, with Lupin lying on the sand and Sherlock about to deliver the fatal blow with a wooden sword. But when I started singing, they suddenly stopped. I noticed they were listening, but I finished the aria I was singing anyway.

When I finished, the only sound on the beach was the lapping of the waves.

"Do it again," said Sherlock in a low voice.

"Yes," said Lupin. "Please do it again! Sing!"

I blushed as much as I ever had in my life. I took off the wig and stammered, "But — but I don't . . ."

"Do it again," repeated Sherlock, leaning on his wooden sword. He looked at me with an almost burning intensity.

I tried to come up with some excuse. "I don't know what to sing."

"You've got a beautiful voice," said Lupin. Sherlock didn't take his eyes off me.

I couldn't take it anymore. I felt exposed as the sound of the waves grew intolerably loud. "Boys, stop it!" I cried. "You're embarrassing me!"

They both saw I was serious. Sherlock shrugged, then helped Lupin to his feet. The three of us went back to acting and trying out the makeup, but it wasn't the same as before.

Eventually, we shared a snack of bread and herring. Lupin produced an odd little knife with a razor-sharp blade from his pocket. With it, he sliced the bread, telling us that a friend of his father had made the knife. He never went anywhere without it. He said his father's friend was now the rich owner of the famous Opinel knife company.

Once the sun began to light up the horizon, we started back home, walking barefoot along the beach. The gulls scurried away in front of us, as the waves broke beside us, now long and regular.

"Have you ever taken singing lessons?" Lupin eventually asked.

"My parents sent me to them for a while," I admitted as I gazed out to sea. "But I didn't think that those senile, old singing teachers were right for me."

I'd known how to sing since I was little, but preferred to keep it to myself. I liked singing, but it was hard to perform in front of other people. My mother had forced me to take singing lessons, which I'd hated. With their fluted handkerchiefs, black jackets, and flabby fingers on the piano, all those posturing teachers would do is repeat for hours, "Do! Re! Mi! Now an octave higher!" She was trying to make me sing in a way that felt completely unnatural.

"I've never heard anybody sing like that!" said Lupin.

"Oh, please!" I said.

"It's true!" Lupin said. "You tell her, too, William!"

Like always, Sherlock was walking a few steps ahead of us. He lifted a hand and said, "I can hear that you lack discipline," he said in a neutral tone.

"What do you mean I lack discipline?" I snapped. He looked back at me over his shoulder.

"If you weren't undisciplined, why would you hate something useful like singing lessons?"

"I hate them because they're boring!" I said.

"Exactly," Sherlock said. "You're undisciplined, like I said."

"Look who's talking!" I snapped.

Sherlock finally stopped walking. "What a temper you have! We compliment you on your voice and you tell us to stop. And if we say you're singing sounds undisciplined because you don't take lessons, you get offended."

Lupin laughed. I didn't. While Sherlock talked, I'd noticed something was lying on the beach just beyond some rocks. It looked like a bundle that the sea had washed up onto the beach, but it made me feel cold inside.

A squawking seagull made me jump, and I realized I hadn't heard a single word Lupin and

Sherlock had been saying. "I'm sorry," I murmured. I grabbed Sherlock's arm and pointed to the strange object on the shore. "What's that?"

They both turned. "My word," mumbled Sherlock, suddenly stiffening.

"*Mon Dieu!*" exclaimed Lupin.

We started running down the beach toward it. When we reached the thing, we saw that it was a man.

Chapter 6

THE BEACH TERROR

We stopped a few feet from the body, just behind the rocks. The man had long hair and was lying face-down in the sand. He almost looked asleep. He was wearing a jacket, a long-sleeved shirt with cuff links, velvet pants, and one shoe. Everything was soaking wet and covered with sand.

"You stay here," Sherlock told us. He bounded over the rocks in a single leap.

"Be careful," I said, but Lupin shushed me.

Sherlock took a few cautious steps toward the man. He looked closely at him, walking around him, before he spoke. "He's dead."

I felt my cheeks go pale. "Dead?"

"Dead," Sherlock repeated.

Lupin began to climb over the rocks. "Wait!" I said, and stopped him. We looked at each other. I didn't want to the left alone, but I had even less desire to get any closer to a dead body than I already was. Lupin's eyes, however, were sparkling with curiosity.

"I'm coming with you," I said finally, somehow able to find some courage. We climbed over the rocks to Sherlock.

The boy who would one day become the greatest detective of all time was kneeling beside the body. He was examining by repeatedly poking it with a piece of driftwood.

"What are you doing?" asked Lupin.

"Trying to figure out who he is," Sherlock said. "Or, rather, who he *was*."

"Shouldn't we turn him over?" Lupin asked.

"Turn him over?!" I cried. "You shouldn't even be touching him!"

The two were now side by side. I put a hand over my mouth and began to look around uncomfortably. "Boys, I really don't think that . . ." I muttered. But they obviously weren't listening.

"Expensive shirt, turned-down collar," Sherlock observed, carefully pushing at the man's clothes with his stick. "Those kinds of things are hard to come by around here."

"Yes, he's wearing very expensive clothes," Lupin agreed. "Look at the cuff links."

"Boys!" I insisted.

"Maybe he fell off a ship," Lupin continued.

Sherlock shook his head. "He's not dressed for being on board a ship. This is more like a business suit."

Lupin leaned over to look at the man's face. His beard was untrimmed, but he also had rather refined features.

I couldn't stand it any longer. I started pacing back and forth, following a kind of crazy zigzag path across the beach. I couldn't understand how they could be so calm. My heart was pounding in my chest, and my face and hands felt icy cold, but they seemed as relaxed as two doctors performing complex surgery in an operating room.

"Boys, we have to call someone!" I said, my voice trembling.

They just continued to discuss something

between themselves. I sighed and stepped closer to them. "Lupin, Sherlock? What —?"

I saw that Sherlock had searched inside the man's jacket pocket with the driftwood and had pulled out two large stones and a soggy piece of paper. It was a note. Lupin picked it up. I put my hands over my mouth. Although the ink had run, you could still read what was written on it.

"'The sea will wash away my guilt,'" read Sherlock.

I stepped back and looked around again. But this time I saw someone at the other end of the beach. He was wearing a blue cloak that completely hid his face and was standing in front of the trees between the beach and the trail we'd followed that afternoon. He seemed to be looking straight at us.

Terror washed over me like a wave. I pointed at him and screamed with all my might, "Let's go!"

Lupin and Sherlock sprang to their feet. I wasn't sure if they'd also seen the hooded figure, but my scream had certainly frightened them. All three of us started to run as fast as we could along the beach, and we didn't stop until we reached the gates to the town.

Once we were there, we leaned up against the stone wall, which was still warm from the late afternoon sun, and let ourselves slide down onto the ground, all of us panting.

"What happened?" asked Lupin, when he finally managed to catch his breath.

"There was a man," I said. "A man wearing a blue cloak with a hood. A hooded man by the trees."

Sherlock closed his eyes. "Are you sure?" he asked.

I nodded, still gasping for breath. "He was looking at us. At us and the dead man."

"The man with no name," said Sherlock. He opened his hand. He'd brought the note they'd found in the dead man's pocket.

Thoughts swirled through my mind like swarms of mad bees. What should we do? Who should we tell? Had anyone else seen us? And who was the mysterious figure who'd been spying on us?

"We do nothing," said Lupin, as if he'd been reading my mind. "We do nothing and say nothing. We were never at the beach. We didn't see a body."

"Our footprints are all over the sand," said Sherlock.

"The tide's coming in," Lupin said. "It will cover them."

Sherlock nodded. "But the fact remains that someone saw us," he said, pointing in the direction of the beach with his chin. "And they were undoubtedly close enough to see our faces."

"We're not sure anyone was even there," Lupin said, briefly glancing at me.

"He was there!" I insisted. "I'm sure of it!"

"You're probably right," Sherlock said.

"So what do we do?" I asked. "We have to tell someone!"

Lupin shook his head. "No. We'll wait to see if the hooded man says something. Otherwise, we don't do a single thing."

"And you think the man I saw will tell someone?" I asked.

Sherlock stood up, casting a long shadow over us both. "Lupin's right. If this mystery man goes to the police, within a few hours everyone in town will know about it all anyway."

"And if he doesn't?" I asked.

"Well, in all probability, Irene, it will mean that you've just seen the murderer," he concluded grimly.

I couldn't breathe for a moment. Sherlock's breathing was as calm and steady as ever. But his eyes burned like shadowy pits.

"And he saw all three of us," I said, finishing Sherlock's thought.

Chapter 7

THE TALKING
WARDROBE

The next day was Friday. I remember that morning perfectly. I got out of bed and looked at my face in the bathroom mirror. I looked like a ghost. I'd spent the whole night tossing and turning, and hadn't slept a wink.

"Miss Irene?" Mr. Nelson said, knocking politely on the door. He entered and handed me a towel and a basin of hot water. "Your mother is waiting for you at breakfast."

"I'll be right down," I lied, keeping my face down so my butler wouldn't notice my tired eyes.

He put the bowl on the edge of the marble top and stood looking at me harder than I could stand. "Are you feeling well, Miss Irene?" he asked.

"I'm very well!" I answered, and then asked him to leave me alone. But I immediately regretted treating him so rudely when I saw that there were rose petals floating in water. A thoughtful touch.

I quickly washed with the too-hot water to get my blood flowing. I rubbed and rubbed with my towel until my skin was all red. I put on a long, light dress that would cover as much of my skin as possible, and then went down to breakfast.

"Irene," my mother said, greeting me. She looked up from the little green leather-bound book she'd been reading for the last few months. "You look awful."

"Thank you, Mama," I answered. "I think it's the sea air." She closed her book, annoyed once again at my insolence. I noticed that despite reading this book for months, her bookmark was still in more or less the same place.

Mr. Nelson timed his entrance to perfection, interrupting our angry silence with a silver tray piled with hotcakes, butter, jam, and a teapot producing wisps of jasmine-scented steam. He served us with his usual courtesy, as if it were a perfectly normal day.

"What does today have in store for us, Horatio?" my mother asked.

He held the now-empty tray to his chest like a shield and answered, "There's a great deal of commotion in town today, ma'am."

I stiffened.

"Commotion?" Mother asked. "Why a commotion?"

"There has been an unfortunate event," answered Mr. Nelson.

My mother's bell-like laughter rang through the room. "Now really, Horatio! Please don't be so dramatic! Just tell us what's going on."

"Nothing that would be appropriate to discuss at breakfast, ma'am," Mr. Nelson said with a little bow.

Mr. Nelson's lack of willingness to talk in front of me confirmed my suspicions. Someone had to have found the dead man on the beach. My mother, however, couldn't have known anything about the reason for Mr. Nelson's reluctance to talk and thus became annoyed. "Please tell me anyway, Horatio," she said sternly.

"On the shore," said our butler, sighing, "a castaway was found, ma'am. They say he was not from the town."

I took a deep breath, thanking Mr. Nelson with all my heart for his vague answer.

"And why should this create a commotion?" my mother asked him.

"Because the gentleman in question was dead, ma'am," Horatio replied flatly, then left the room.

The discovery of a dead man on the beach was more than enough justification for my mother to send an urgent telegram to my father. She scurried away to do just that.

* * *

A little later, I saw Mr. Nelson putting on his bowler hat to go to the post office in town. "Mr. Nelson?" I said. "May I come with you?"

"Surely, Miss Irene," he said.

I thanked him and followed him out the door.

"So," I said as we walked along the street, "what did you hear about what's happening in town?"

"These things are not appropriate for the ears of a respectable young lady," he said matter-of-factly.

"That's ridiculous," I said. "Do you think that

respectable young ladies are so stupid that they don't need to know about what's going on around them?"

"Not at all," he answered.

"So, why don't you want to tell me?" I asked. "Is it because you think I'm just a girl? Maybe because I'm too young?"

"One or the other," he said.

"Mr. Nelson, it won't take me long to find out the story on my own, anyway," I said plainly. "Look around you — it's the only thing anyone in town is talking about."

It was true. Along the streets of Saint-Malo, people were gathered in groups and talking excitedly. Quite often, one would point toward the beach.

"You can always ask your new friends, Miss Irene," Mr. Nelson said with a smirk.

At the post office, there were around thirty people standing around in little groups. Of course they were talking about the discovery on the beach. I didn't see any threatening hooded figures nearby. But there was one stout gentleman going from one group to the next, asking questions and scribbling in a notebook, most likely notes for an article he was writing for the evening paper.

"Excuse me, excuse me," Mr. Horatio Nelson said as he opened up a passage for us leading to the telegram counter. I tried to listen to as many of the conversations as I could, but all I could hear was total confusion.

"Are you happy now, Miss Adler?" asked Mr. Nelson when he'd finished dictating the telegram. The fact that he'd used my surname meant that he was annoyed by the situation.

I looked at him. "A crime has been committed," I said, "but everyone who's talking about it makes it sound different."

"That's right, Miss Adler," Mr. Nelson said. "Exactly right. Everyone is talking about it and everyone has their own version of the story. That's why it's best to wait until the truth comes to light."

As we walked home, I felt strangely empty and troubled by what I'd heard at the post office. My heart had jumped at everything, scared that someone was about to mention that three children had been spotted on the beach, poking at the corpse. Fortunately, no one did.

Then again, the fact that no one had mentioned seeing us on the beach was a bad thing.

"Shall I call you down for lunch?" asked Mr. Nelson as I walked up to my room. I can't remember what I said in response. I was completely lost in my thoughts.

I lay down on my bed and looked out my window. Suddenly, I heard a voice coming from my wardrobe!

Chapter 8

A STRANGE GUEST

Well, my wardrobe wasn't talking, as much as it was whispering. And it was whispering my name. "Irene? Irene?"

My first reaction was to pinch myself. But the whispering was soon followed by a sharp knock on the wood, a rustle of clothes, and someone cursing quietly.

"Lupin?" I asked, recognizing his voice. I jumped out of bed, walked over to the wardrobe, and yanked open the door.

Lupin stared back at me. "What are you doing

in there?" I asked, feeling rather embarrassed. I remember thinking that this was probably the first time a boy had set foot in my bedroom. It was certainly the first time a boy had been hiding in my wardrobe.

My blue silk dress was tangled around Lupin's head. It draped over him like a cloak. "Shh!" he said. "They'll hear us!" He seemed almost annoyed by the fact that I was surprised. "Sherlock and I are here to check on you."

Hearing Lupin calling his friend by that name made me happy, but I didn't let it show. "But why are you in my wardrobe?!" I snapped.

"Shh! Don't you get it?" Lupin said. "We're checking to see how safe you are!"

"Safe?" I said, putting my hands on my hips. "Safe from what, may I ask?"

Lupin finally freed himself from my dress, threw it down all crumpled in a corner, and motioned that he wanted me to move so he could climb out of the wardrobe. "We don't even know who saw us yesterday on the beach," he explained.

I didn't move. He could stay stuck in there — I wanted him to explain himself properly before I let him out. "And that's a good reason to sneak into my bedroom?" I said.

"Even a baby could have snuck inside, Irene," he said, pointing at the unlocked window.

I looked at the open window with the sun pouring through. I hadn't even considered the possibility that someone would try to hurt me. "I always sleep with the window open," I mumbled.

"That's what Sherlock told me," Lupin said. "That's why I had to come and see if you were in any danger. And I'm sorry to say it, but the answer is yes."

I squinted at Lupin. "Sherlock really said that?" I asked. I'd never told anyone where my room was. How could Sherlock have known? The only possible explanation was that he'd spied on me, which irritated me. But the thought also made me smile. I sat back down on the bed.

"Sorry I scared you, but I wanted to get away before you realized I was here," said Lupin. "But then I heard you come back home and I thought it was better to hide."

"Was Sherlock snooping around my house trying to find out which room was mine?"

Lupin just stared at me. "Have I missed something?" I asked, suddenly blushing.

"Oh, no! I'll go back the way I came in," Lupin said, pointing to the window. "I've got to go meet William — er, Sherlock — on the walls."

"I'm coming with you," I said. But as I got up off the bed, I realized that I had a snake coiled around my ankle!

I screamed like a baby. Lupin grabbed the repulsive creature and pulled it off me, throwing it against my bedroom door. But I couldn't stop screaming.

Mr. Nelson came running up the stairs before everyone else and threw the door open. He saw me standing on the bed pointing at the poor snake, which was now looking for some corner to escape to. At that point, it was probably much more frightened of me than I was of it.

But Horatio Nelson wasn't scared at all. He grabbed the poker from the fireplace. I asked him not to hurt it, so he simply grabbed the snake and set it free in the garden. I felt like that queen who'd mercifully pardoned her attacker. I began to breathe more calmly and, little by little, I settled down.

"Is he gone?" asked Lupin, peering out.

I despaired upon realizing I'd just reacted like a spoiled little city girl in front of Lupin. I wanted the ground to open beneath my feet and swallow me up.

Lupin smiled. "Your eyes sparkle when you're angry, you know," he said.

Before I could decide whether or not that was a compliment, he climbed out through the window with a rustle of ivy leaves.

Chapter 9

A DEAD MAN'S SECRET

The three of us were sitting in our usual spot up on the city walls, just near the statue of the pirate. Sherlock and Lupin were on the wall, their feet dangling in the air. I was more cautious and lay on my stomach with my chin resting on my hands. The uneven stones of the wall pushed into my skin under my clothes.

I began to wonder why neither Lupin nor Sherlock seemed even a little bit frightened. "Do you think we should be afraid?" I asked.

"Scared of what?" Lupin asked. He didn't even

mention the snake, while I didn't say a word about him hiding in my room.

"We found a dead body on the beach," I said. "Does this mean there's a murderer on the loose?"

"Not necessarily," Sherlock said. "There could be more than one. Or none. Or maybe he simply died of natural causes."

"Natural causes, Sherlock?" asked Lupin. "You saw the state of him. How could he have died of natural causes?"

Sherlock grunted. "Death is probably the most natural event in our lives," he said.

Lupin said, "But the note in his pocket —"

"The note only said that the sea would wash away his sins," Sherlock interrupted. "Maybe it really was a suicide note. Maybe it wasn't. Of course, his pockets were full of rocks, and why would he have put rocks in his pockets unless he was trying to drown himself? Remember, we have no idea who he was. We don't know the cause of his death. We don't even know if he had some reason for committing suicide." Sherlock crossed his thin legs beneath him. "Therefore we don't have sufficient evidence to be sure he was killed, committed suicide, or died of natural causes."

"You're forgetting about the hooded man," said Lupin. "The man with the blue cloak. According to Irene, he was watching us."

"I really did see him!" I said.

"I'm sure you're sure you saw him," said Sherlock. "But we can't be as sure as you are."

I scowled. "Thanks for your trust, Sherlock."

"It's not a question of trust," Sherlock said. "I'd say the same thing even if I'd seen him."

"The man I saw could have been the murderer," I insisted.

"Sorry Irene, but I have my doubts, as well," said Lupin.

"Oh, really! Would you care to tell me why?" I asked.

"Because a murderer would go into hiding," Sherlock said. "He'd try not to be seen. Even if it was only by three kids like us."

"Good point," I admitted. "I just wish we knew more."

"We're the only ones who have seen that note,"

Lupin said. "And we've got a clue that no one else has — not even the police! I say that we investigate this ourselves."

"Are you sure?" I asked him. "That note was disturbing. You really think we should . . . ?"

Sherlock shook his head. "Maybe we should just give it to the police."

Lupin threw his hands into the air. "Oh, yes, let's be good little children. We'll hand the evidence over to the police and go back to playing games. Don't you want to find out what happened?"

Sherlock looked at me, then at Lupin. Then he laughed.

"What's so funny?" Lupin asked.

"I'm laughing because it all sounds impossible," Sherlock said. "Dangerous and impossible."

"You don't even want to try?" I asked.

"I didn't say that," Sherlock said. "But think about it. Even with the note, it will be very difficult to find out who the man was, where he lived, and what he was doing here. Not to mention the possible dangers of poking our noses into a potential murder."

"Are you scared?" Lupin asked, a grin dancing across his face.

Sherlock laughed again. "No, not in the least!" he said.

Lupin relaxed a little. "Now that's the Sherlock I know! How about you, Irene? What do you think about it?"

"I think it's crazy. No one's talking about anything else in town. I saw a journalist at the post office. And then there's the police . . ."

Lupin scowled. "Chief Inspector Flebourg?" he said. "My father says he's an utter fool! He spends half his day eating and the other half sleeping. He won't get in our way."

"Yes, but what about everyone else?" I asked. "Everyone in town is interested in this case."

"Irene is right," said Sherlock. "The more people who stick their noses into this, the more likely they'll trample all over the clues."

Lupin clapped his hands together rapidly. "Well, then we'd better get moving!"

"I'm in," I said. "But where are we going?"

Sherlock looked at us. Our determination seemed to amuse him. "Where most of the history of this town starts and finishes," he said, jumping to his feet. "The harbor!"

Sherlock and I hurried away. We'd almost reached the path that wound down from the ramparts to the old part of the town before we realized Lupin hadn't moved an inch.

"What are you waiting for?" I asked Lupin. "After all that effort put into convincing us, you just stand there like a statue?"

Lupin stared at us with an enigmatic smile. He seemed to enjoy being mysterious. He certainly enjoyed being irritating.

"Would you mind telling us what's going on in that head of yours?" I asked, walking back to him.

"What if I said that there's someone who knows who the dead man is?" Lupin said.

I rolled my eyes. "Simple," I said. "I'd ask you if you know who this someone is."

"Maybe I do," Lupin answered. He walked up to us, dancing around us like some kind of ridiculous ballerina. "Last night, I couldn't stop thinking. I kept asking myself who the dead man could be. The question kept going through my head so much that I couldn't get to sleep. We know from his clothes — the jacket, the cuff links — that he was very well dressed and probably wealthy. People like that don't go unnoticed around here. But this morning, when everyone started talking about the dead man, the whole town agreed on one thing —"

"That they'd never seen him before," I said.

"Exactly," said Lupin, snapping his fingers. "Which means he wasn't from around here. And if he wasn't from around here, he was either here on vacation or just passing through. So, this morning I went to all the best hotels in town." Lupin grinned widely. "At the Maritime Hotel they couldn't tell me anything helpful." Sherlock looked like he was about to say something, but he remained silent and let Lupin finish. "But at the Hotel de la Paix, I think I found out something."

"Ah," Sherlock said finally.

"My father's friend works there," Lupin added. "I asked him a few questions and discovered that the dead man was staying with them. Apparently he came and went all the time for business."

"And does your father's friend know his name?" I asked, too curious to wait for the rest of the story.

"*Mais oui!*" Lupin said triumphantly. "The dead man's name is François Poussin!"

I was so excited by what Lupin had discovered,

and the ingenious way he'd done it, that I hugged him then and there and complimented him on his good work. Then I noticed that Sherlock hadn't moved a muscle or said a single word. It looked like something was bothering him. I began to wonder if he was jealous of Lupin, or if maybe there was some sort of contest between them to impress me . . .

That memory still makes me smile. I obviously didn't know Sherlock Holmes very well at that point! I changed my mind the second Sherlock finally decided to speak.

"That's all quite remarkable," Sherlock said. Lupin unwrapped himself from my arms. "Remarkable and very unusual." He began to look more and more thoughtful.

"Unusual?" Lupin said. "What's so unusual about having a room at the Hotel de la Paix?"

"Oh, nothing at all," Sherlock said. "There's absolutely nothing unusual about the man having a room at the Hotel de la Paix, particularly if he's from out of town." His mouth curled in an expression of doubt. "But I also did some investigative work this morning, since I'd come to basically the same conclusions that you had." Sherlock made another of his long pauses for effect. "And the funny thing is, I tracked him down as well — but his name was Jacques Lambert and he had a room at the Hotel des Artistes!"

Chapter 10

HOTEL DE LA PAIX

There must have been something predestined about our lives. What other explanation could there be for how three children who'd just met in a remote seaside town would get involved in such a strange and mysterious crime? Perhaps fate wanted the three of us to share a memorable adventure that would link us for the rest of our lives.

After all, how could anyone even imagine a more incredible story than ours? One man found dead on the beach. A man who had two different names and rooms at two different hotels in the same town. And another, no less mysterious man who was spying on us when we found the first man's dead body.

To top it all off, there was now a possibility that Lupin's father's friend, the one who worked at the Hotel de la Paix, was trying to confuse us even more. I can't remember exactly what his name was. Something Dutch, I think — Van Hesselink or something like that. What I can remember is how his name just didn't match his appearance. He was a small man with round eyes who wore a jacket three sizes too big for him. To talk to him, you had to speak into his good ear or he couldn't hear you.

We asked Lupin's father's friend about the man he knew as François Poussin and he responded with a series of jumbled sentences. "Ah, Mr. Poussin, of course. He was one of our guests. A handsome man. Very tall. Although not too tall. A handsome man, indeed. Not that it's my place to say whether or not our guests are handsome, but he really was. Maybe even more handsome than your father, Arsène. That says it all, don't you think?"

We kept questioning the man and eventually found out that Poussin had been staying at the hotel sporadically for almost a month. "He was never here for more than three days at a time. Each time, after three days away, he'd come back again. His leaving and going was like clockwork."

Sherlock asked to see the guest register, but apparently the hotel didn't keep one. "Did he ever leave a handwritten note?" he asked.

"What?" the man asked.

Sherlock rolled his eyes. He and the man went back and forth a few times to clear things up. Sherlock wanted to find something written by François Poussin so he could compare it with the note we'd found on the body at the beach. We eventually convinced the man to let us see his room.

"You never spoke to him?" asked Lupin, as we all went up a creaky staircase in single file.

"Never!" roared the man. "Apart from a few words here and there, like I said. But nothing important. He'd just ask me for a coffee or a fruit juice."

"Did he have an accent?" I asked.

He stopped in his tracks at the top of the stairs. "An accent, you say, Miss? Well, now that I come to think of it, yes, he had an accent. A southern accent.

I'd say he was from Marseilles, maybe." He fumbled with a master key. "I'm only doing this because your father and I are friends, you understand."

The little man turned to Lupin. "Don't you touch or move anything, you hear?!" he warned. "Actually, just stay near the door and look inside." Finally, he opened the door.

"Have the police already been here?" asked Lupin, sliding past the man and into the room.

"Not since I've been on duty," the man answered shortly.

"All the better for us," Sherlock said.

"Please, Arsène!" the little man said. "I'm doing this as a favor to you. Don't make me regret it." The little man then launched into a muddled discussion about something which none of us paid much attention to.

That Friday had been all about bedrooms to that point. It was the day Lupin had hidden himself in mine, scaring me half to death. And now we were in the bedroom that was apparently the last place where the dead man had slept.

The moment I set foot in that room, I felt

overwhelmed by anguish. And there was something else. Something vaguely gruesome. I carefully avoided touching anything and moved as stiffly as a puppet as the man rambled on and my two friends carefully inspected everything.

Sitting on the nightstand beside the neatly made bed was a small red book. There was also a jacket, a pair of velvet pants, a small suitcase, bed linens, and a pair of shoes.

Sherlock lifted the shoes and turned them around in his hand. "It's only slightly used," he said, noting how the leather sole was barely worn.

There was practically nothing in the room. There were no clues as to what work the man did, no business cards, nothing that could put us on the right track to learning more about him. When I looked at the bedside table again, however, I noticed that the little red book had disappeared . . .

Soon after, the little man took us down to the lobby hotel. "And you have no idea who might have killed him?" Sherlock asked the porter, the floor creaking beneath our steps.

This time the porter heard the question the first

time it was asked. "At least ten people have asked me that today," he said with a shrug. "He never had any visitors. He never talked to anyone — at least not that I know of. He was always coming and going. And I have no idea what kind of business he was in. He washed his own clothing, so he never spoke to any of the staff here. As far as I know, he was killed by the Rooftop Thief."

My eyes went wide. "The Rooftop Thief?" I asked. "Who's that?" I had to repeat the question until the man's face changed shape into a kind of grin. He probably meant to look mysterious, but it was actually rather funny.

"Oh, a lot of people have seen him," the porter said in a playful voice. "On nights when there's a full moon, a figure moves around on the rooftops all dressed in black. The dark figure climbs the walls like a spider!" I glanced at Lupin, expecting a Cheshire-cat grin, but found that his face had gone entirely pale.

* * *

Later that evening, I was walking home with Sherlock. It seemed as if the dark sea beside us had swallowed up all of the colors in the town. The streets seemed gray, the stone houses appeared black, and the wisteria hedges vaguely silver. We'd talked a lot about the man with two names but didn't reach any conclusions.

"This Rooftop Thief," I said, breaking a long silence. "Do you think he was the man I saw on the beach?"

Sherlock didn't seem very convinced — I could see it in his eyes. And he hadn't believed a single word of what the porter had told us.

"I don't know," Sherlock said. His perplexed expression told me that I shouldn't push the issue.

I noticed that Sherlock had chosen an indirect path to my home that didn't pass by his house. Perhaps it was because he was walking me home, and not the other way around, or because he didn't want me anywhere near his family. Whatever the reason, I was grateful.

"It's getting late," I said when we were almost back to my house. "I hope your mother won't be angry."

It took a few seconds for Sherlock to understand what I'd said. When he did, he chuckled. "I'd finished all my chores before I went out. I'm not worried. When she's playing cards, she's usually back home late at night."

"Can I ask you something?" I asked. He stuck his hands in his pockets. "Did you take it?" I didn't have to explain what I was talking about.

"Only to see if he'd written anything in it," Sherlock said.

I nodded. "His handwriting. Of course," I said. I sighed deeply as we turned the last corner.

"Lock yourself inside," Sherlock said as we approached the door of my home.

"What?" I asked.

"Double check the door, even though you have a butler," Sherlock said. "And make sure to close your window." He looked up at my house and I noticed that he was eyeing the two lighted windows on the first floor. "Lupin told me that one is yours," he muttered, pointing to one.

I lifted an eyebrow. "Oh, really? He told you that, did he?" *Which one of them actually figured out which was my window?* I wondered.

Sherlock looked at me with sparkling eyes. He

was about to say something but, whatever it was, he changed his mind at the last moment. "Good night, Irene," he said instead. "I'll see you tomorrow."

"Good night, Sherlock," I said.

I watched as he passed into the darkness. When I turned back to my house, I noticed that Papa had arrived.

Chapter 11

VOICES IN THE NIGHT

"Irene!" Papa called.

He waited for me in the hall with his arms wide open. I threw myself into them. "When did you get here?" I asked.

"Just now, my little one!" Papa said.

My father lifted me up in the air, as he'd done even in my earliest memories of him. He only put me down when my mother immediately chastised him. "Leopold!" she shouted. "Put her down!"

That was what she always called my father. It made him sound like some Bohemian prince. And he would have made a good prince, although he didn't quite look like one. He was quite short and tubby, with intelligent eyes and a mustache that seemed to be in a perpetual state of agitation. His hands were soft and strong at the same time, and he always smelled like cologne — even after his longest journeys.

I saw immediately that he was very tired, and that surprising me like this had taken a lot of effort on his part, but I could tell he was happy to be there all the same.

"So how's your vacation going?" he asked.

"I know you already know!" I said, then leaned in close. "It's as dead as a doornail." I added with a whisper and a grin.

"I know, I know," he answered, rustling my hair. "It's all quite scandalous, this murder business, isn't it?"

There was a real trust between me and my father I sometimes hardly know how to explain. He'd just arrived a moment ago, and I already wanted to take him to meet my new friends, and maybe even to see Ashcroft Manor.

Instead, we went into the dining room. We were

greeted by an array of fine crystal and silverware —
and a guest. He was a tall, thin man who was about
sixty years old. He was very distinguished-looking.
I was told his name was Dr. Morgoeuil and that he
was a doctor in the town. Mother had invited him so
he could meet Father, although Dr. Morgoeuil would
speak very little that evening.

My parents had an unusual way of entertaining
guests. Mama did most of the talking, while Papa
simply added one-word comments here and there.
Sometimes he just nodded. Then, from time to time,
he'd shoot a quick glance at me. I never missed them
because I knew exactly when they were coming. It
was always when he was sure that no one else was
looking. Father took advantage of these moments to
make funny faces at me. He'd feign being shocked at
something that was said, or he'd stick out his already
big lips in a comical pout. Or he'd pretend that he
was starting to fall asleep. He was always funny, and
I loved meals when we all ate together — especially
because it didn't happen very often.

As my mother explained to Dr. Morgoeuil, my
father was a very busy man who looked after trains
and railways for the Bavarian royal family. He was

a very important person. But he traveled so much that he envied people who were able to just stay in one place and enjoy the peace and quiet of their own hometown. In all likelihood, those same people envied him for his life of constant first-class travel and his extended stays in luxury hotels.

"Absolutely fascinating discussion, Mr. Adler," said the doctor. "And thank you, Mrs. Adler, for the meal. Everything was delicious."

The adults then went to the drawing room for coffee, tea, or wine (which I wasn't allowed to touch). I said goodnight to them, beginning with the doctor and ending with Papa.

"Would you like to go the beach tomorrow?" Father suggested.

"Are you staying with us for a while?" I answered, both excited and doubtful.

"Only until Monday, little one," he said. Now that Father was home, I suddenly forgot all about the hooded man on the beach, the snakes hiding in the ivy, and anyone who might be spying on my house from the dark alleyways of the old town.

Maybe that was a mistake on my part, because none of those things forgot about me.

★ ★ ★

I awoke with a start in the middle of the night. The first thing I saw was my wardrobe — the door was ajar and I thought I could hear someone whispering inside. My heart was pounding.

"Lupin?" I asked, stupidly.

Of course no one answered. I got up and walked cautiously over to the window, pulled back the curtains, and looked out. I saw the dark sea, crossed by the jagged, silver sliver of the moon. The sky was so clear that you couldn't possibly have counted all the stars. There was no one in the street. No shadows behind the wisteria. Everything seemed quiet.

With my heart in my throat, I opened the wardrobe door. But inside there was nothing but the black shapes of my clothing.

Then I heard it again. Whispering. I realized it was my mother and father. I looked out into the hallway. The grandfather clock chimed dully, the sound seeming to come from the far reaches of that the dark sea. I could only hear some of what my parents were saying — only when one of them raised their voice.

I don't know why, but I decided to listen to them.

Maybe it was because I was so absorbed by my role as an investigator that I thought I had to investigate everything. Perhaps I was just curious. Or maybe I just wanted to sit up all night talking with Father in the sitting room. Whichever reason it was, I stood at the top of the stairs listening to them, using my imagination to fill in for the words I couldn't quite make out.

There was one thing that wasn't difficult to understand: they were talking about me. "I'm worried," I heard my mother say.

My heart started beating faster. What was she worried about? The man on the beach? Something else?

"There's no need to be worried," my father answered quietly. "It will be calmer here than anywhere else."

"Maybe so," she said. "But people will talk."

"Let them," Father said. "The doctor . . ." I couldn't hear the rest of the sentence.

"He'll never know, will he?" Mother asked.

My father hesitated before answering. "I think we should tell him sooner or later," he said.

I could guess what they were talking about. I

had an urge to go downstairs and tell them that I understood, but just then a hand appeared on my shoulder and gave it a gentle squeeze. I opened my mouth to scream, but didn't make a noise.

"I think it would be best if you went back to bed, Miss Irene," whispered Mr. Nelson. He'd come up behind me without me even noticing. "It's not appropriate to listen in on other people's conversations."

In the darkness, all I saw was his white smile, like a crescent moon. I followed his advice, and the next morning I'd forgotten all about what had happened.

Chapter 12

THE DARK LADY

"Care to tell me where you've been?" Sherlock asked me the moment I stepped onto the porch of Ashcroft Manor. I smiled, glad to see him even though he seemed annoyed with me. He walked toward me, but then passed right by and headed down the trail which I'd just come.

"Come on, let's go!" he said.

I scoffed. *Who does he think he is?* I wondered. *And who does he think he's talking to?!*

"William Sherlock Holmes!" I exclaimed, not budging an inch. Hearing his full name in that tone of voice had exactly the effect I'd hoped for. He jerked to an abrupt stop. "Apologize to me immediately!"

"What?!" he snorted. "Apologize for what? For waiting all morning for you to arrive?"

"But my father's here!" I said, although I still felt guilty for having kept him waiting.

"So?" Sherlock said.

"So . . . I haven't seen him for a long time," I said. "We went for a boat ride!"

"And how was I supposed to know that?" Sherlock asked.

"Why did you need to?"

"We've made a pact, the three of us!"

"A pact?! What are you talking about?"

"We're involved in an investigation, young lady!" Sherlock said. "A dangerous investigation! Or have you forgotten already?"

"How dare you? You're not my brother!" I shouted. "And you're certainly not my . . ." I didn't know what I wanted to yell at him, but that unspoken word was like magic. We stopped arguing at that point, suddenly realizing I was standing just a couple of inches from Sherlock's face. We both blinked twice.

Sherlock narrowed his eyes and said, "Well, I . . ."

And I said, "I just mean to say . . ."

There followed other embarrassing attempts to explain ourselves, made up of unfinished sentences that I won't bother to share.

Luckily Lupin arrived shortly after to break it up. "Big news!" he cried. I'd never been so happy to see the third member of our small club of amateur detectives.

We went and sat on the broken, old furniture on the old porch of Ashcroft Manor. In front of us was the sea. Behind us, the wind whistled through the empty rooms of the house. We shared a bag of little breadsticks called *grissini* that Papa had brought back from Paris for me.

"Perhaps we were wrong to ignore what we heard about the Rooftop Thief," said Lupin. "Apparently he struck again last night."

"Someone else is dead?" I asked, startled.

"Hold your horses," he said. "It was a burglary!"

"Oh. What kind of burglary?" I asked.

"A diamond necklace was stolen from Lady Martigny," said Lupin. "It was very valuable, too, according to Chief Inspector Flebourg! You should have seen him, he was hopping all over the place!"

"How did you know?" asked Sherlock.

"I heard about it secondhand," said Lupin, his face nearly buried in the bag of breadsticks. "This morning the chief inspector visited my father at work." At this point, Lupin gave me a long look that made me feel uncomfortable. "For a consultation."

I gulped. "What sort of consultation?"

"An acrobatic consultation," Lupin said with a chuckle. "To get into Lady Martigny's house, the Rooftop Thief climbed down off the roof, but it was steep and dangerous. And he must have been very good at his job, since he didn't leave a trace behind — not on the walls, the other roofs, or even on the window."

"And was the window open?" Sherlock asked.

"It seems it was, yes," Lupin said.

"And what did your father say?" I asked.

"To the chief inspector, you mean?" Lupin shrugged. "He told him that to get through that window, the thief must have been a real professional and there's probably no chance of catching someone like that. But later, after the inspector was gone, my father said that he couldn't have done a better job himself!"

We all laughed. At that time, none of us — not even Lupin — knew what his father's real job was. We all thought he was a master juggler, a martial arts expert, or a circus performer. We were soon to discover that there was much more to him than all that. And Lupin would eventually follow in his father's footsteps . . . and become much better than even he was.

"But do you think there's some connection between the theft of the diamond necklace and the dead man on the beach?" I asked. I broke a breadstick into three pieces and gave one to each of us.

"A thief isn't a murderer," said Lupin. "But it's still odd that in a small town like Saint-Malo that two things like this would happen in such a short space of time."

"Certainly, the burglary makes things more complicated," said Sherlock. "The chief inspector not only has to find out what happened to the man on the beach, but now he has to solve the theft of a diamond necklace. Do you know this Lady Martigny?"

Lupin shook his head. Sherlock pulled the little red book he'd stolen from the hotel nightstand out of his pocket and opened it.

"Have you discovered something?" Lupin asked him.

"Yes," he answered. "The note that we found in his pocket wasn't written by him." He thumbed through the book and showed us some words written in the margin of a page. It was strikingly different than the handwriting on the note.

"This complicates things," said Lupin, sounding more intrigued than annoyed.

"Well, it certainly makes the suicide hypothesis less likely," Sherlock said. "But why would a man be carrying what looks like a suicide note in his pocket that he obviously didn't write himself?"

I couldn't help but think that there was indeed some connection with the Rooftop Thief, but kept that thought to myself. "So?" I asked anxiously. "What do we do?"

"First of all, we've got to take the book back to where it belongs," Lupin said, taking the book from Sherlock. "And then we've got to go to the other hotel where he had a room: the Hotel des Artistes."

"Was there anything else interesting in the book?" I asked.

"A playing card that he used as a bookmark,"

Sherlock said, showing the card. It was the Queen of Spades. He quickly put it back in his pocket. "An obvious reference to Lady Martigny."

"Obvious?" I repeated in surprise. "How so?"

"People call her the Lady in Black," explained Sherlock, "because she always dresses in black as if she were in mourning."

"I've heard of her," Lupin said. "And I've also heard that she's married to a rich man who prefers his business to her, so he's often away." I bit my lip, thinking of my own family.

We stayed there, sitting outside Ashcroft Manor for a little while longer as we came up with a thousand different hypotheses about the recent events. We got along very well together. We were three peas in a pod, excited by the sounds of our own voices. And none of us questioned whether our friendship was right or wrong.

The time we spent together on that porch flashed by, all three of us overwhelmed by our unending curiosity. We were happy, restless, and fearless. We were playing with the lives of other people with utter recklessness. Perhaps it was because life hadn't yet begun to play with us.

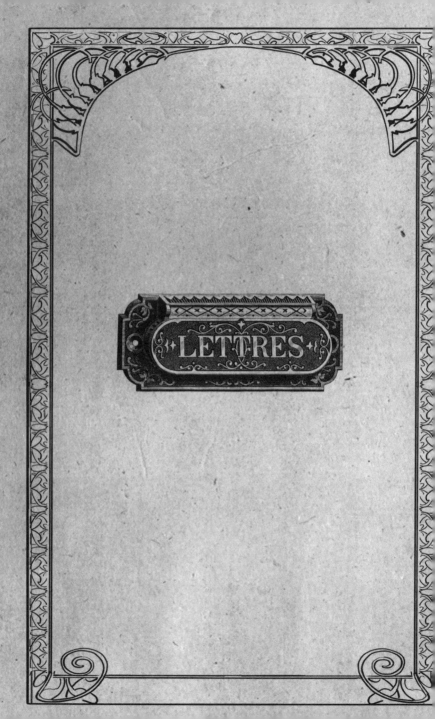

Chapter 13

HOTEL DES ARTISTES

We decided to head to the Hotel des Artistes next. Despite its name, there was absolutely nothing artistic about the hotel. It was an old, gloomy, and soulless building near the harbor. Although it was an establishment of some prestige, there was something seedy about it.

And as you approached the reception desk, it almost felt as though people were hiding among paintings while spying on you.

The desk clerk was tall and hunched over. He stared at us through thick glasses and seemed to jerk like a puppet whenever he moved. He didn't seem to care about why we were so interested in Lambert and told us a story that was very similar to the one we'd heard at the Hotel de la Paix. Mr. Jacques Lambert constantly came and went, staying in his room for no more than two or three days at a time.

"Did he ever meet anyone here?" asked Sherlock. "Did he receive a lot of correspondence?"

The man with the glasses sucked through his missing teeth before answering. "Let me think. Did he meet anyone? No. He mostly stayed in his room. As far as correspondence goes, my little, pushy friends, perhaps you should ask the gentleman over there. Isn't that right, Octave?" He said the name rather loudly to make sure the nearby man heard him.

Behind us, Octave lowered the newspaper he'd been reading with a rustle. "My, look who's here," he muttered staring at us with a bored expression. "Am I wrong, or are you Mr. Holmes?"

Sherlock turned. "Sir," he said, very politely.

"Yes, yes, it is you," Octave said. "How are things at home? Are things a little calmer now?"

I saw Sherlock grow agitated as he did whenever anyone mentioned his family. "Everything is . . . quite calm now, thank you, sir," he replied flatly.

"I'm happy to hear it," said Octave.

Just then I recognized him. I'd seen him the day before at the post office with Mr. Nelson. As I discovered later, he ran the post office. "What are you looking for, children?"

The man at the desk answered for us: "They're asking about Mr. Lambert's correspondence."

"Mr. Lambert's correspondence?" the postmaster said. "Why on Earth would you be interested in such a thing?"

"No real reason," answered Sherlock. We didn't know if anyone else yet knew about the dead man's double identity and we didn't want to be the ones to reveal it to the world.

"We're playing Catch-a-Thief," Lupin suddenly announced, trying to sound younger than he was. "We heard about the diamond necklace getting stolen and wanted to help find it."

The postmaster chuckled. "And you think you'll find it in a hotel?"

The desk clerk drummed his fingers on the desk. He had long, curved fingernails that reminded me of some tropical seashells I'd once seen in a museum in Paris.

"Well, it must be somewhere, right?" Lupin said calmly.

"And you suspect Mr. Lambert?" the postmaster asked. "Well, as police go, you're not too bad. However, I'm afraid I'm going to have to disappoint you. You see, Mr. Lambert is —"

"Dead, we know," I blurted out. The postmaster and the desk clerk exchanged a long look, which made me feel terribly uncomfortable. Sherlock and Lupin suddenly went stiff as well. Perhaps we'd been naive to ask for information so openly.

"I'm afraid I haven't had the pleasure of meeting you yet," said the postmaster.

"Irene Adler," I said. "I'm on vacation in Saint-Malo."

"And you arrived at the wrong time, it seems," the postmaster said. "On behalf of my town, I can only apologize for this unpleasant situation. A suicide on the beach and a major theft — and only a few days apart!"

"It's just what those filthy journalists thrive on!" the desk clerk declared.

"It's strange you should say that," said Lupin. "Because Lambert was apparently a news correspondent for a paper in Le Havre or Brest. Which is why we're interested in his correspondence."

The desk clerk seemed genuinely surprised by this information. Lupin's completely false piece of information made the postmaster sit up in his seat.

"A newspaper correspondent?" the postmaster asked. "Really?"

"It's the first I've heard of it," said the man at the reception desk. "But that would explain his constant comings and goings."

"I could check the postal records," muttered the postmaster, who was obviously growing more and more intrigued. "But that's strictly between us, of course!"

"Of course!" we all answered in unison, smiling at him like the good little children he likely expected us to be.

We stayed there a few minutes longer chatting to the two men, but didn't discover any really useful information apart from the various rumors and opinions they'd heard around town. Nothing we didn't already know. But listening to those two blather on did give us a good idea of what the people of Saint-Malo thought about the recent happenings. Most people were indifferent, and bordering on annoyed, over the suicide of Poussin (also known as Lambert). And conversely, most people were delighted over the thief who'd made a fool of Lady Martigny.

"Those diamonds were quite happy under the ground before they went and dug them up and made them into a necklace!" the postmaster said with a wicked grin. "You're only asking for trouble if you show them off to the world like that."

"By the way, have you ever heard of the Rooftop Thief?" asked Lupin. The question seemed to echo among the statues of the dark, dusty lobby before it got an answer. I heard a door slam followed by the sound of someone scurrying away.

"He's one of the many legends of this town," said the desk clerk after a while. "I've heard stories about him since I was a child."

The postmaster shrugged. "Whenever anything

a little strange happens around here, you can be sure that someone will start talking about the Rooftop Thief."

* * *

"A newspaper correspondent?" Sherlock asked Lupin as soon as we were far enough away that we could laugh about it. "Le Havre! Brest? How on Earth did you come up with all that?"

Lupin chuckled. "I don't know! It just popped out."

"You were great," I said. "And now that lovely postmaster will help us with our investigations!"

"Well done," Sherlock agreed. "But we have to be careful. We're not the police. People might get suspicious."

"Suspicious?" I repeated. "Of what? We're just three children asking a few questions."

"Yes, but there are still too many unknowns about this whole thing for us to let down our guard," he insisted. "Even forgetting about the Rooftop Thief, who is apparently nothing more than a myth anyway, there's still the hooded man who saw us on the beach. There's also the person who stole Lady

Martigny's necklace. And, of course, another person who murdered Poussin, a.k.a. Lambert, a.k.a. the dead guy on the beach."

"Assuming that they're not all the same person!" added Lupin.

"Do you have another stroke of brilliance to share, Lupin?" I asked with a playful smile.

"Perhaps I'm having a good day," he said. "Let's make the best of it!" He threw his head back in laughter. In that moment, Sherlock looked quite admirable with his fine features, and eyes so bright they looked like gems.

We walked at the pace set by Sherlock's long, rhythmic strides. Like always, he was two steps ahead of us. In the warm sun with the cool breeze coming in off the sea, it seemed that nothing could stop the three of us. While I was with those two, I felt ready to take on anything. But once we'd passed the last houses and reached the harbor walls, our sense of invulnerability suddenly vanished.

A shabby-looking boy stood haloed in the light that flooded the street. He made a movement that made me realize he was waiting for us. Sherlock suddenly stopped. Lupin stared at the boy and then at me.

I saw two more figures appear from nowhere. "What's going on?" I asked in alarm.

What was going on was that we were trapped.

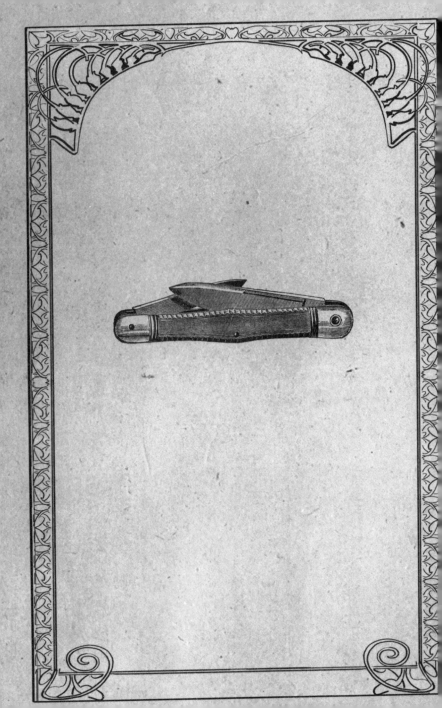

Chapter 14

AN EVENTFUL DAY

"Hey, hey, hey!" yelled the boy who'd appeared in front of us. "Look who we've got here. The three little detectives."

We stopped in our tracks. Sherlock stood in front of me, Lupin two steps to my side.

"Stay calm," muttered Lupin. But the way they were both standing around me as if guarding me from harm, I felt anything but calm. We'd been ambushed by thieves who loitered around the harbor. You could tell by the clothes they wore, how they shuffled their feet, and simply by the way they moved. I counted them, trying not to look at them. There were five of them at first, but soon two more appeared from another alley.

"Just three little busybodies," the boy said with a nasty grin, "who don't know their place." He spat on the ground and came toward us, stopping about three paces away.

"And who might you be?" asked Sherlock.

"Who might I be?" the bully said. "Did you hear that! He asked me who I might be!" The bully's eyes seemed to shine with a malicious light, feeding off his companions' laughter. "You really want to know who I might be?"

"No," Sherlock said coldly. "Not particularly. But I would like to know what you're doing here."

"What *I'm* doing here? This is my town," said the boy, sticking his chin out. "Not yours."

"If you say so," Sherlock said.

"That's exactly what I say. And I'll also say that I've been hearing a few rumors around town recently."

"I'm not really interested in gossip, but if you insist on sharing," answered Sherlock, still unruffled.

"They say that for a few days now, some snotty-nosed kids have been asking too many questions. They've also been seen snooping around on beaches."

I looked up suddenly. *The hooded man I saw on the beach!* I thought. *Could it just have been one of these fools?!*

"You must really be stupid to go around trying to dig up trouble like that!" continued the boy, who was apparently the gang's leader. His comment prompted more laughter.

"You think we're stupid, do you?" said Sherlock. "Well, it's obviously not us you're looking for then. Goodbye." Sherlock started walking, but the second he did, the boy jumped like a spring and blocked his path.

"Not so fast!" he said. "There's no rush."

The rest of the gang immediately came up close and surrounded us. I felt Lupin's back against mine. "Stay calm," he whispered. "Don't worry. Don't look at them."

"Who do you think you are, beanpole?" the leader asked Sherlock, two steps ahead of me.

"I'm not a particularly interesting person, I can assure you," Sherlock answered coolly.

"But you do interest me!" said the bully, coming even closer. "You interest me and my friends!"

"I warn you," said Sherlock with his teeth

clenched, "you're making a big mistake if you don't let us go."

"It seems to me that you're the ones making the big mistake, beanpole!" growled the other. "We saw you. We know what you did."

My heart stopped beating. What was he talking about? The dead man on the beach two days ago?

Sherlock just shrugged.

"We know that you've been sniffing about the Hotel des Artistes," the leader said.

"Really?" Lupin said loudly, speaking for the first time. "Who told you so? Was it Spirou, the kitchen boy?" The smallest of the bullies stood straight up, obviously surprised that Lupin knew his name. "I didn't even know he knew how to talk," said Lupin with a laugh. "I thought he could only grunt. Sherlock, did you know Spirou could talk?"

"Someone told me he could, but I didn't believe it," Sherlock answered.

Two of the bullies chuckled in spite of themselves, while Spirou stuck out his chest, trying to look as aggressive as possible. But the leader gestured to them and everything in the alley went quiet. Seagulls squawked in the distance.

"You should be more careful," said the ringleader. "Stick to playing with dolls. Go and play in the garden. Just stop going around asking questions!"

"Did you hear that, Sherlock?" Lupin said sarcastically. "No more questions."

"It's a terrible pity," said Sherlock, feigning disappointment. "So what should we do now?"

"Just get out of here!" cried the bully.

"But which do you recommend? Dolls or play in the garden?" Lupin said, then he burst into laughter.

"Maybe you don't understand me, but this is no joke!" growled the boy.

"But you look like one!" Sherlock said.

"He does, doesn't he!" Lupin nodded. "A joke that isn't even funny."

I turned to look at him in astonishment. And so did the bully. "What did you say?" the bully said. "You're calling me a joke?!"

"Well, you obviously are," Lupin said calmly. "You and all your friends,"

"Yes, I'm sorry, but I do have to agree. You're not even particularly good at being bullies," said Sherlock.

There was a metallic *click*. Something flashed in

the shadows. The bully had pulled a shiny knife out. "You don't seem to understand who you're dealing with," he said, lifting the blade up to Sherlock's face.

"On the contrary," Sherlock answered, as calm as ever. "You don't seem to understand who *you're* dealing with."

Out of nowhere, Sherlock threw an overhand punch to the thug's face. The blow was so powerful that it knocked the boy to the ground almost instantly.

The seconds that followed seemed to last an eternity. Little Spirou and another thug hurled themselves at Lupin and knocked him to the ground with a fast punch and a kick. Sherlock instantly kicked the knife out of the lead bully's hand and then charged the two remaining bullies, his fists flying.

Out of the corner of my eye, I saw the leader struggling back to his feet. "You stay where you are!" I cried, delivering a well-aimed kick. He collapsed back onto the ground without a sound.

"Let's get out of here!" cried Lupin. By this stage, the kitchen boy, Spirou, had run off and Lupin was left with only one opponent. I watched Sherlock. He stood up to the two thugs like a professional boxer.

He held his fists up in both attack and defense, had his legs slightly apart, and was shifting his weight from one foot to another while dodging every punch they threw at him. Or at least most of them. But when one of them delivered a hard punch to Sherlock's chin, I couldn't keep my eyes open.

"Irene!" Lupin cried. My eyes opened to see him dispatch his remaining opponent with a quick one-two punch combination. He then grabbed me by the arm and dragged me to the top of an alley.

"But Sherlock!" I cried, turning to our friend, who was still fighting.

"He'll look after those two all by himself, don't you worry!" Lupin laughed, pulling me along. But I wriggled away. For a moment, it looked like the two thugs were getting the upper hand.

"Sherlock!" I cried and instinctively ran to him. I didn't see the carriage coming. The coachman pulled hard on the reins. The horses' hooves missed me by just a few inches. The driver was now standing and waving his fist at me. Behind the glass in the carriage I saw a woman's face. She was all dressed in black, and looked both sad and elegant.

All this lasted only an instant. When I turned back

to look at Sherlock, I realized how wrong I'd been about him needing my help. One of the thugs was running away while Sherlock punched the other one repeatedly.

Lupin grabbed my arm. "What did I tell you, Irene?" he said. "He's fine! Come on, let's go!"

This time I let him lead me away, and we started running at breakneck speed through the streets of Saint-Malo. Lupin held my hand tightly and led me through dozens of twisting, turning alleys without ever slowing down.

After we finally slowed down, my heart felt like it was about to burst and there was a dull pain in my chest. Lupin, however, was laughing.

"What's so funny?" I asked between breaths.

"Well," he said, with hardly even a hint of breathlessness, "that was fun!"

"Fun?! Being threatened at knifepoint by a gang of criminals is fun!?" I cried.

"Criminals? Them? They wish!" Lupin boasted. "Did you see how easily we took care of them?"

"Yes, but, Sherlock — we left him alone!"

Lupin nodded. "But it was more important to get you out of there."

"I know how to take care of myself, thank you!"

Lupin laughed. "I think the one you kicked would agree with you there! He'll have your boot mark on his cheek for quite some time!"

Lupin looked at me with those deep, sparkling eyes. He said nothing for a moment. Then he pulled me close to him.

"Lupin?" I said.

"Yes?" he said.

I grabbed his chin and turned his head until he finally noticed that three more thugs were sprinting toward us.

Lupin sighed. "And where did they come from?"

"I don't know, but what do we do now?" I asked.

"We put our backs against the wall," he said.

The three came boldly toward us, taking up the whole width of the narrow, sun-flooded alley.

I don't know why, but until then I'd always imagined that things like this only ever happened at night. Or in novels, like Robert Louis Stevenson's books.

Lupin let go of my hand. "Don't worry," he said, standing between me and the thugs. "I'll take care of this."

Lupin threw back his shoulders, lifted his fists, and ran at the thugs screaming like a madman. I suppose he was trying to scare them. And for a second, it seemed to work. The three stopped and exchanged a puzzled looked. But they were soon over their surprise and came at him more aggressively than ever. Lupin stopped in his tracks and took a half step back uncertainly.

Three against one . . . he's doomed! I thought.

But I was wrong. A dark figure suddenly appeared behind the thugs. He grabbed two of them and effortlessly threw them up against the alley wall. The third thug was so surprised by the attack that he froze, unsure of whether to attack Lupin or run from the newcomer.

"Mr. Nelson!" I cried. I ran toward him. By this point, Lupin was fighting with the last thug — a muscular boy who obviously knew how to fight. He and Lupin traded a few hard punches, then Lupin jumped back to dodge a punch and ended up right beside me. He shot a glance in my direction. The intense expression on his face vanished for an instant, and he smiled. "Get out of here! Go on!" Then he threw himself back into the fight.

Mr. Nelson kneeled down in front of me like I was still a child. He looked straight into my eyes. "Are you all right, Miss Irene?" he said quietly.

I nodded, staring back. Where had he come from? How had he done it? He took my hand and walked me past the two thugs he'd knocked down and took me away from the alley. "Mr. Nelson, Mr. Nelson," I said in a panic. "What about my friends?!"

I saw his huge shoulders lurching in front of me as he led me away. "Oh, don't worry about them, Miss Irene. From what I saw, I believe they can handle themselves."

Chapter 15

A MESSAGE

The church bells were ringing. It felt as though they'd always been ringing. I rolled over in bed, listening to the beat of my heart as it echoed in my ears along with the bell.

Without moving, I counted ten low tolls followed by two higher ones. That meant it was ten-thirty this Sunday morning.

"Lupin," I said. And then, "Sherlock!"

I slid out from between the sheets and looked out the window. Huge, slow, gray clouds were covering the sun. I could hear my parents chatting happily about something downstairs. My mother laughed, and it calmed me a little.

I just hoped that Mr. Nelson hadn't told them anything about what had happened the day before. I quickly washed, put on a light dress, and tiptoed down to breakfast.

"What a beautiful smell!" I said with a smile. "I couldn't resist coming down any longer!"

"Irene!" Mother cried. "What's wrong with your hair?"

I ran a hand through my hair and I realized I'd completely forgotten to comb it. It must have been standing up all over the place.

With a laugh, Father ruffled it up even more. "Your mother and I couldn't decide whether to come and wake you up or not."

I bit into a still-warm bread roll. It was like a door to my stomach suddenly swung open. After a long, tense night, I was famished.

"It is not proper for a young lady of your age to spend so much time in bed," said Mother, as prim and uptight as ever. If only she'd known what this young lady had been doing the day before. How I'd helped fight off a gang of thugs. How my two friends had battled them hand to hand. And how we'd been rescued by Mr. Nelson!

As if he could sense my thoughts, Mr. Nelson came into the room. The giant butler carefully avoided exchanging even the slightest glance with me. He poured me a cup of tea and exchanged a few words with Father. "Today I suggest you don't go boating, sir," Mr. Nelson said. "The sky is dark and the seagulls are flying low."

Father sighed. The bad weather had arrived with diabolical precision, making it all the more likely that instead of going out in a boat, we'd end up taking tea somewhere in town that Mama considered to be, as she put it, "suitable for our family."

"Do I have to come, too?" Father asked Mama, both confirming my suspicions and proving that they'd already discussed it.

I took a long, slow sip of tea, enjoying the warmth and sweetness as it cascaded around my mouth and then down my throat. "Will Lady Martigny be there?" I asked.

"Pardon?" asked my mother.

"At tea today," I said, taking another sip.

"The lady who suffered the theft," Father reminded her.

"I know who Lady Martigny is," she replied. "But I wasn't in charge of the invitations for the tea this afternoon."

"Such a pity," my father said to me. Then he made a funny face that almost made me spit my tea out all over the table.

"Irene!" said Mother, jumping to her feet.

"I beg your pardon! I beg your pardon!" I quickly said, then gulped down the last of my tea, excused myself, got up from the table, and ran out of the room. "I'll see you later!"

As I left, I heard my mother say, "Leopold, did you see that? I really think that we should . . ."

My father must have shushed her because I heard him say, "You're mistaken. We don't need to do anything at all." I was so lucky to have a father like him.

"Miss Irene!" Mr. Nelson called after me from the garden door as I was about to open the gate out into the street. Dressed in his elegant butler clothes with his starched cuffs, it seemed impossible that he was the same person who, just the day before, had saved me from a group of thugs.

"What's wrong, Horatio?" I asked.

I saw him hesitate. It was the first time I'd ever called him by his first name. I'd hardly noticed myself doing it. It had come so naturally. I was wondering whether I should apologize or say nothing, but finally decided to retrace my steps back to where he was standing. I spoke again before he could respond. "I want to thank you for yesterday afternoon."

"Oh," he said. "There's no need, Miss Irene."

The bells began to strike eleven o'clock, and Mr. Nelson and I waited patiently for them to finish.

"I wanted to say to you, Miss Irene," he said, "that if today you intend to go looking for your friends . . ." I nodded. That was precisely where I was going. "Then I think you will find them just outside the town, at the old barracks."

The news surprised me. That was where Lupin and his father lived, but I'd never been there. Like Sherlock, Lupin seemed to spend as much time as possible away from his home.

"Thank you, Horatio," I answered. "But how did you know?"

"This morning when I went into town for the shopping," Horatio said, "I met Master Lupin at the bakery, Miss."

"And how was he?" I asked.

"He seemed well. He told me to give you the message that today he and Sherlock will be at the old barracks."

"He really told you that?"

"Yes, Miss Irene. And then he added 'for training.'"

"Training? For what?"

"This he did not tell me, Miss Irene."

I nodded. "Thank you, Mr. Nelson,"

"Or Horatio?" he said, with a barely perceptible smile. "I have no objection to you calling me Horatio, if you wish."

"How about Horry?" I said with a smile.

He immediately raised a hand. "No, Miss Irene. I do not think it is appropriate to overdo these things." Our smiles grew into shared laughter.

I walked back to the gate. As I opened it, I looked back one last time. I wanted to know how Mr. Nelson had managed to show up at just the right moment the day before in the alley. I wanted to ask if it was just good luck.

But when I looked back toward the house, Mr. Nelson had already gone back inside.

Chapter 16

THÉOPHRASTE

I soon arrived at the barracks. The townsfolk of Saint-Malo continued to call it the "old barracks" since no soldiers had set foot in the place for many years. Judging by the condition of the walls and an old tower nearby, it probably hadn't been used since the battles between Napoleon and Lord Wellington. It was just outside Saint-Malo, but still so close to the wall that it really was still a part of the town. It overlooked the sea where Ashcroft Manor stood, near where we'd found the body of the dead man. A narrow lane led from the main road to a large, sunny courtyard, where a few chickens were scratching the dirt.

"Is anyone here?" I asked, looking toward the windows that were overgrown with ivy. "Lupin? Sherlock?" The only response I heard was clucking. When I moved closer to the house and crossed the area where the chickens were, they squawked and ran off.

"Anyone home?" I called again.

I saw an enormous, wild tree beside the road. It spread out over the courtyard and pushed up against the wall of the building with its long, gray and white branches. Its leaves created a flickering mesh of shadows on the gravel.

"You must be Irene," the tree seemed to say as I walked by.

Then I noticed that there was a man high up among the branches. He was crouching like a cat with his hands resting on his knees. His feet were bare. He had a wiry, slender body and a ponytail of black hair tied back with a black kerchief.

I shaded my eyes with my hand to see him better. "Good morning," I said after a moment.

"Good morning to you," said the man, with a smile that I recognized instantly. He had the same open and warm smile as Lupin.

"You must be Théophraste!" I exclaimed, immediately putting one hand over my mouth. "I'm so sorry. I meant to say Mr. Lupin. I beg your pardon!"

The man in the tree laughed loudly and then climbed down the tree quicker than I thought possible. In no time at all, he was standing on the ground next to me.

"You can call me Théo, if you like, young lady," he said. "So . . . are you the Irene that my son keeps talking about?"

My cheeks instantly turned the color of a tomato. "Well, um, yes," I muttered. "I suppose I am."

"I thought so! Come on, then," he said. "The boys are out back." I followed him without hesitation, watching his bare feet tread lightly upon the gravel. I followed him inside. We went through a curtain over the doorway and into a huge sitting room piled high with books and exotic-looking objects.

Soon we found ourselves on a veranda that

overlooked the sea. I glanced around and saw a big jade lion and a Tibetan gong. Two elephant tusks were on the wall, crossed like swords.

"Arsène told me about what happened yesterday," said Mr. Lupin.

"Really?" was all I managed to say.

"He said that the three of you had a lucky escape from those thugs."

I nodded, not knowing exactly what to say.

"And do you know why it was lucky?" continued Théophraste Lupin. I shook my head. "Because you haven't had the proper training."

We stepped off the veranda and the man led me to where my friends were. Sherlock was wearing white bandages on his fists and was punching a large bag hanging from a length of rope.

Lupin also had gauze on his hands, but he was pushing up against the bag, making it continuously spin around. After a few more punches, they swapped places.

"Fighting, Miss Irene," said Lupin's father, "is an art. Just like music or dance. You need to study hard and apply yourself. Nothing can be left to chance."

I laughed awkwardly, wondering what would happen if my mother ever heard any of this.

Lupin's father spotted my embarrassment immediately. He visibly stiffened. "Do you find it embarrassing to be here, Miss?" he asked. "Or perhaps you felt it was rude that I greeted you from the top of my meditation tree?"

"Oh, no! Not at all!" I said quickly. And I meant it. "It's just that it never occurred to me that punching people could be an art!"

Théophraste crouched down so that I was a little taller than he was. Neither Lupin nor Sherlock had even noticed us and continued to punch the bag. "It's because you only see the surface of the thing, Miss," he said quietly in that tone of voice people only use for important things. "Every movement of the body can be an expression of grace, energy, or balance. It's all about the harmonious use of the body."

"Healthy mind, healthy body," I murmured.

"Exactly," he answered. "From what Lupin tells me, I'm convinced you have an excellent mind, Miss Irene. And I've rarely seen a prettier face than yours."

I blushed again, even redder than before. I had

never met anyone who talked so openly. It amused me and made me feel quite nervous at the same time.

"But the question is," he said, "how much is your body capable of?"

I stiffened as something pressed between my shoulder blades, which was immediately followed by a stinging sensation. I spun around with a jerk and moaned with pain.

Lupin's father held up a single finger, showing it to me as I massaged the base of my neck. "With proper study of one of the Oriental martial arts, you don't need anything but a single finger to make a whole gang of bullies turn and flee."

I didn't know what to say. If the Lupin family wanted to make an impression on me, they'd more than succeeded!

He got back to his feet. "I believe my son and young Master Holmes are expecting you."

"One day I'd like to learn how to do what you just did," I said.

"I'm always here, Miss Irene. Here or meditating in the plane tree!" he said with a grin.

I returned his smile and walked over to my

friends, trying to ignore the small but insistent pain that still ached between my shoulders.

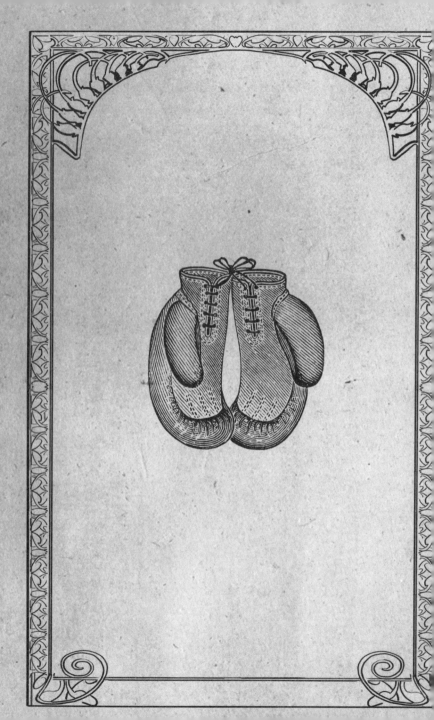

Chapter 17

ALL FOR ONE

The fight with the thugs the night before had taken its toll. Sherlock had a black eye and a cut on his upper lip. Lupin had a cut on one arm and a nasty bruise on his side that made him move quite stiffly. They were both shirtless and covered in sweat. Lupin had a sculpted frame, while Sherlock was awfully thin. The veins on his biceps and hands stood out against his pale skin.

Sherlock started taking the bandages off his fists, but I stopped him. "What are you doing?" I asked. "You're not stopping for my sake, are you?" He stared at me, breathing hard, his temples throbbing. I turned to Lupin. "Have you got some of those bandages for me, too?"

Lupin laughed and stared at me, wide-eyed, until he realized I was serious. "I've never punched anyone in my life," I said. "Maybe it's time I learn how, don't you think?"

Before answering, Sherlock stuck his jaw out and spat a rough mouthguard out into his hand. "You'll always be safe with us," he said. "It's just that yesterday, we were taken by surprise."

I smiled at him. "I'm fine, thanks for asking," I said.

"I can see that," Sherlock answered.

"While you, on the other hand . . ." I began.

"I'm absolutely fine as well," Sherlock said.

"Your gloves, Irene," said Lupin, passing me some bandages. "Give me your hands. I'll show you how to wrap them."

Lupin carefully wound the bandages around my hands over a layer of cotton wool. When he'd finished, I beat my fists together. I noticed that Théophraste was watching us from the veranda. So, just like a perfect show-off, I sauntered up to the punching bag without asking for anyone's help and threw the first punch of my life. I put all of my strength into it. Sure enough, the punching bag didn't move an inch but the pain in my hand was sheer agony!

* * *

Later that day, we were sitting in a circle, all of us exhausted from jumping rope, punching drills, and all the other exercises that Lupin had made us do. All we had the energy to do was talk, and that suited me just fine.

"There's only one thing we know for sure," said Lupin. "Well, two things actually." As usual, Sherlock didn't seem convinced. "The first is that we now know there are people from here, from Saint-Malo, involved in the recent crimes — not just people from out of town like we originally thought."

"And the second?" I asked.

"They want us to know they were involved," Lupin said.

"You mean those bullies yesterday? Who were they?" I asked.

Lupin and Sherlock shook their heads. "Apart from Spirou, we have no idea," Sherlock said.

"But they know who we are," I said. "And they

also seem to be well organized. It sounded like they'd been following us for days."

"I'm not too sure about that," said Sherlock. "Maybe they'd just heard from someone that we'd been asking questions at the Hotel des Artistes, or something."

I then remembered the sound of someone running the day before in the hotel lobby. I told them since it seemed to support Sherlock's theory.

"Spirou is the only one I recognized," said Lupin. "He's the dishwasher there. Maybe it was him running off to tell the others, and that fool of a gang leader decided to ambush us —"

"Maybe," Sherlock interrupted him. "Or maybe the gang leader only works for someone else, and that someone else told him to give us a scare."

"Someone else?" I repeated. At this point, I was sure that Sherlock knew more than he was saying. "Someone else who?"

Sherlock shrugged. "Maybe someone who's more important and more dangerous than the bully," he said. "Someone who actually might be involved in Lambert's death or the theft of the necklace."

"I'm not sure you're right," said Lupin. "But if

there is someone behind it all, we've just sent him a pretty clear message!"

I agreed. The gang probably thought they were dealing with some silly children who they could easily scare off. Instead, they found two seasoned fighters and a willful young woman. But it was also true that if Mr. Nelson hadn't come by when he had, we probably wouldn't have been sitting there talking among ourselves with little more than a few bruises.

I massaged my aching fingers. I didn't like boxing, but I was glad I'd tried it. I felt lighter and faster than before. "Do we have a plan?" I asked. Everything we'd figured out seemed to make sense, but it hadn't helped our investigations one bit.

"Spirou," Sherlock simply said.

"What do you mean?"

"He's the only member of the gang we know," said Lupin. "And he's possibly also one of its weakest links. I don't know how involved Spirou and the others are in all this, but they do seem to know more than we do."

Sherlock drew a series of lines in the dirt with a dead twig. "We also know where he lives. His father is a fisherman and they have a little house at the harbor. We'll follow him and see what he does when he's not working at the hotel."

"If he leads us to a den of thieves and they're talking about Lambert or, perhaps, stolen necklaces," Lupin said, "then we've solved the case!"

I shook my head. "That sounds dangerous. What if they see us?"

"No one will see us," said Lupin. "We'll wear disguises. And anyway, Sherlock is very good at following people without them noticing."

"And Lupin's just as good as I am," added Sherlock.

I looked at them, thinking about my bedroom window and which of the two had secretly followed me. Maybe they both had, but without telling each other. The idea made me smile for some reason.

"There's no saying that this Spirou will immediately take us where we want to go, though," I said. "It could take a while."

"We could take turns," suggested Lupin, getting immediate approval from Sherlock.

"All right. So which one of us will go first?" I asked. My friends stared at me with stunned expressions. I turned my palms up and looked into their eyes. "Um, what did I say that's so odd?"

"No way, Irene, you can't —" began Lupin, but I silenced him with an angry gesture. He stared at the ground.

I couldn't believe it! This was the sort of condescension I would have expected from my mother — not from my new friends. Enormous anger welled up inside me. I took a deep breath and tried to blow it all out of me. "Listen closely, you two." Sherlock timidly tried to interrupt me, but I signaled to him to be quiet. "I have no intention of repeating this. We started this adventure together. The three of us: Sherlock, Lupin, and I. We even made a pact the evening we found the body. We decided that all three of us would try to find out what had happened. We knew it would be dangerous, and maybe that was the reason we did it."

"Don't be so silly," Sherlock said with a cutting tone. "The way you're talking, you make it sound like we're the Knights of the Round Table!"

"Maybe we are," I said. "If not, then what are we? Just children?"

"Irene, I —" began Lupin.

"You what, Lupin?" I interrupted. "If my butler hadn't helped you last night, what would you have done with three thugs on top of you? And you, Sherlock, have you finished cooking lunch and dinner for your family yet so your mother can go off and play cards with her friends? Do you really think you two are so much better than I am?"

I was furious, but I regretted what I'd said the moment after the words had left my lips. I took a deep breath. "The three of us made a pact, didn't we? Have you forgotten already? So let's stick to it." I got up, holding my bandaged hands out in front of me. "Either all three of us finish this thing together, or none of us do." I avoided looking at them. I kept my eyes straight ahead, staring at the sea. I held my arms stiff to stop myself from shaking.

Lupin got up first. He put his hand on mine and said, "You're right. I'm with you. All for one and one for all and all that nonsense."

With a sigh, Sherlock got up as well. He put his hand on top of Lupin's. It was so big that I could feel his fingers wrapping right around mine as well. "You're both crazy," he said.

"Say it, Sherlock," I hissed, refusing to look at him. "All for one and one for all."

He stood there shaking his head for a long time. "All for one and one for all," he said finally.

But Sherlock was probably right. We probably were crazy.

Chapter 18

A WALK IN THE DARK

I awoke in the middle of the night to a sound. At first I thought it was one of those unexplainable little noises you hear at night in old houses. Then I realized that someone was throwing pebbles at my window. I ran over to open it.

"What is it?" I asked in a whisper. I felt like I was talking to the night.

"Irene?" someone answered from the moonlit garden. "It's me!"

"Lupin?" I said. "What's going on?"

"It's Spirou! He's on the move!" he said.

"Spirou," I mumbled. I wasn't properly awake yet

and was finding it hard to understand anything. All my thoughts seemed to be moving lazily around in my head. "I'll be right down," I said finally.

I went to the bathroom and groped around in the dark for the dress I'd worn earlier that afternoon. I heard the ivy rustling against the wall of the house. When I turned, Lupin was there, silhouetted against the bright night sky.

"Lupin!" I almost screamed, hiding behind the door. "What are you doing?!"

He threw me a bundle of clothes that landed on the floor at my feet. "It would be better if you put these on," he said, before disappearing back the same way he'd come.

I burst out laughing. *Like father, like son,* I thought.

The clothes were for a boy: a pair of corduroy trousers, a shirt, a beret, and a pair of shoes. Although they were well worn, they smelled quite clean. I put everything on as quickly as I could, then went to my door to listen. There wasn't a noise, except for Mr. Nelson's even, gentle snoring.

I leaned out the window, trying to figure out how to climb down. I took a deep breath. "Come on, Irene!" I whispered to myself. "You can do this.

I hoisted myself up onto the windowsill and looked for a foothold, stretching a leg deep into the ivy. Fortunately it wasn't too hard to find one. I left the window ajar and, staying close to the trunk where the branches were the strongest, I carefully climbed down. It was almost impossible to see the branches with the leaves reflecting the moonlight like the scales of a big fish.

Somehow I managed to make it down to the lawn. I ended up grazing my hand and an elbow, but clenched my teeth into a smile so I wouldn't look like a crybaby. Lupin was waiting for me just beyond the rose garden. I saw his eyes sparkling in the darkness. "Let's get going! Sherlock is waiting at the harbor for us," he said.

Together, we made our way through the streets. Lupin was in disguise as well. He was wearing what looked like shapeless rags, which were much less sweet smelling than mine, a floppy, old sailor's hat, and a long, fake beard that made him look vaguely ridiculous. I followed him without saying a word. The shoes he'd given me were horribly tight and the shirt made it difficult to move.

We went down to the harbor, then up onto the

ramparts. "He should be here somewhere," Lupin muttered, as we traveled from shadow to shadow.

But Sherlock wasn't where we were supposed to meet him. There was nothing but a dried bean, its white skin glowing in the moonlight. *He's moved,* I thought, picking up the bean. Immediately, I spotted a second bean a few feet away. I picked it up, too, and showed it to Lupin. "He's left a trail for us."

"Spirou must be on the move again!" said Lupin.

We followed the trail of dried beans and soon found ourselves skirting the ramparts and passing through the huge gate back into the town. We followed the walls, trying to avoid the few people who were still out and about. The church steps seemed ivory and silver in the light of the moon. The old bell tower cast a shadow over the square like a giant spear. We kept moving, looking like shadows ourselves. We descended a steep, crumbling flight of stairs, turned down a lane, and passed under a dreary row of arches that looked like the ribs of a giant skeleton in the dim light.

Suddenly a hand darted out from the shadows of a side street and grabbed Lupin by the back of his neck. I saw Lupin pull something out from under his shirt — a pistol with a long black barrel. In an instant it was pointed directly at the throat . . . of Sherlock.

"You frightened me!" Lupin said, putting the weapon back under his shirt.

"I heard you coming from a hundred feet away!" Sherlock complained, letting go of his friend's collar. He then gave me a long look. "They suit you," he said, referring to my clothes.

"So does your mustache," I answered, ducking into the shadows of the alley between them. "Did I really see what I think I just saw?"

"What do you think you just saw?" Sherlock asked.

"Don't play games with me," I whispered coldly. "Do you have a pistol, Lupin?"

"It's my father's," he answered. "It's part of his stage act. It doesn't work but it looks real." He handed it to me. "See? It's only to scare them with."

It was surprisingly heavy, with an ebony grip inlaid with mother of pearl. It seemed more like a large piece of jewelry than a weapon. "Scare who?" I asked, handing it back to him.

"We still don't know yet," said Sherlock, signaling us to follow him.

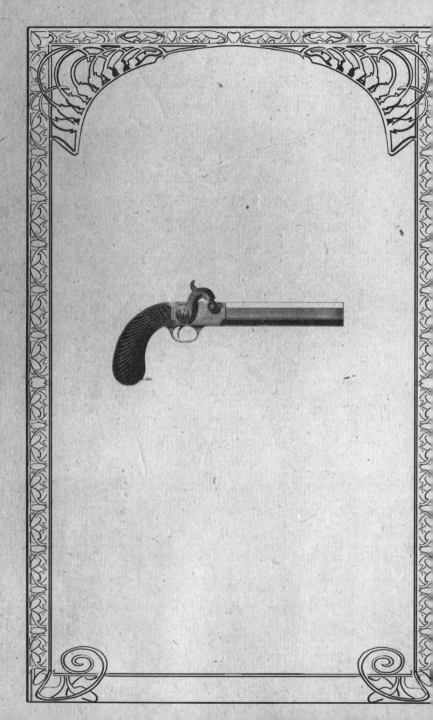

Chapter 19

BEYOND THE DARKNESS

We crouched in a corner that stank of damp and filth. The buildings around us were tall, narrow, and decrepit. They looked like old, half-burnt candles. The massive shadow of the town walls to our left concealed us in darkness.

Sherlock pointed to the other side of the area toward a dilapidated door. I could hardly see a thing at first, but after my eyes adapted to the darkness, I saw the shape of a man guarding the entrance.

"He went in there?" asked Lupin.

"And not alone," Sherlock said from behind us.

"How many?" I asked.

"Since I've been here, four people have gone in," Sherlock said.

"Bad news," said Lupin.

"Not necessarily," said Sherlock. "It looks like there's some sort of meeting going on. Perhaps this is exactly what we need."

We heard the sound of approaching footsteps. A figure was walking toward the door. The newcomer exchanged a few words with the guard, who stepped aside and let him enter.

"Just like the other four," whispered Sherlock.

"Did you hear what they said?" I asked.

"I think it was a password or something," Lupin said, "but I couldn't make it out."

"Sherlock?" I asked.

Sherlock was peering into the darkness. The moonlight caught his nose, making him look something like the figurehead of a ship. "Sherlock, did you hear me?" I repeated.

He nodded. "Lupin, give me the pistol," he said. Lupin handed him the gun, and Sherlock walked across the cobblestone road straight toward the guard. A moment later, Sherlock disappeared into the dark doorway.

"What is he doing?!" I asked Lupin.

"No idea," my friend answered.

Time seemed to stop. My heart pounded harder, then harder still. Just then, Sherlock came out from the doorway and signaled to us to join him. After exchanging a confused glance, Lupin and I walked toward him.

"Quickly, give me a hand!" Sherlock said, then dipped back inside.

A figure was lying on the floor near the entrance. As I neared him, I saw that the man who had been guarding the door was now bound and gagged.

"Sherlock!" I exclaimed. "What did you do?"

"Our friend here is just taking a little nap," he said. "But he'll wake up soon enough!"

Sherlock bent down to grab the man under his arms. Lupin took his ankles. Grunting with effort, the two hid him in an empty room nearby.

"This pistol has a nice, hard grip," said Sherlock, handing the pistol back to Lupin. They both grinned.

We followed a dark hallway deeper into the building. Like always, Sherlock walked ahead of us, avoiding every obstacle and threat as if he could see in the dark. Lupin guarded the rear. Somewhere in the distance, above us on the upper floors, we could hear voices, footsteps, and some laughter. We made our way toward the sounds, carefully climbing a staircase that seemed ready to collapse under our shared weight.

On the second floor, a glimmer of light appeared. "Friends!" a guard greeted us. He was lying on a broken couch with a battered oil lamp beside him that created a red halo of light.

"Friend," Sherlock replied, walking past him with his face down. The lamp threw out just enough light to see the walls. They were decorated with paintings of hunting scenes, and the stucco was ruined by the dampness. I followed Sherlock step for step. Lupin was so close behind me, I could feel his breath on my neck.

The voices grew louder as we neared a strip of carpet on the otherwise bare floors. We checked the doors on the left and right. They were all locked. The hallway turned right. At the end there was a large room lit by a flickering candelabra. We passed several rooms, all of them with gaming tables and old chairs.

It's a gambling house, I realized. *A secret place for people to play illegal dice and card games.*

In the room at the end of the hallway there was a large fireplace with a mirror hanging above it. In the exact center of the ceiling there was a large, jagged hole. A ladder leaned up against the edge of the gap. It seemed as if most of the voices we'd been hearing were coming from there.

Without saying a word, Sherlock climbed the ladder. When he reached the top, he disappeared. Lupin motioned for me to follow.

At the top was a man. I tried to hide my small hands from him. "Are there any more?" he asked in a heavy accent.

I looked down and tried to speak from my throat to lower my voice. "There's one more," I said. The man grunted. He drained a glass of something and motioned for me to climb up.

At the top of the ladder, I saw Sherlock just a few steps away. Lupin and I joined him. We were in a large room full of broken sofas, tattered chairs, and soiled cushions. There was a buzz of voices, with at least twenty people standing around in small groups. Luckily for us, the only light was from a couple of wax-encrusted candles. We went to a dark corner a little ways away from the rest of the people.

The flickering light illuminated the crowd. I saw a bizarre patchwork of elegant clothing and scars, silk scarves and glass eyes, tailored waistcoats and broken noses, starched shirts and unshaven beards. It was like a costume party that had been infiltrated by the most wicked-looking criminals.

I thought to myself that I was lucky that Lupin had woken me with a start like he had earlier that night — my messy hair made me fit in.

The ugly faces, the stench of perfume, the broken furniture, the flaking ceiling, the boarded windows, the long tables used for playing dice games — these elements gave the room a devilish feel. I wanted to squeeze Sherlock and Lupin's hands, but couldn't. So, I simply followed them, trying not to make eye contact with anyone.

I felt suffocated by the musty smell of the room that came from the mildew and the smoke that hung in the air. I shuddered every time I heard a glass or bottle clink, or passed someone who laughed or whispered a prayer for a lucky roll.

I heard a scraping noise and turned to look. The ladder was being pulled up through the hole in the floor. My heart was beating faster than ever. I felt pure, cold fear.

There was no way out.

Chapter 20

A GENTLEMAN'S MEETING

The room suddenly went quiet. The gamblers suddenly stopped their laughter and chatter as if someone had given the order to shut up. Sherlock, Lupin, and I kept close to each other in the darkest corner of the room. We tried to be invisible, like shadows among the shadows. I could barely make out the dimly lit backs of the men farthest from us as they bowed toward someone. Others took off their hats and fidgeted with them nervously. We copied them.

The reason for the sudden silence soon became

clear. A man with a shiny head and small pig-like eyes appeared. He was dressed in a gray, formal suit that was at least two sizes too small for him. The mother-of-pearl buttons on his waistcoat seemed on the verge of shooting off across the room, and his black tie was knotted around his neck like a noose. As the man gave greetings to others, I saw that his fingers were covered in rings. And like the desk clerk at the Hotel des Artistes, he had long fingernails.

He walked to a wooden platform in the center of the room, his trousers stretching at the seams as he stepped onto it. "Welcome, gentlemen!" he said with bravado. "And I do mean gentlemen, since proper ladies are not allowed at our meetings!"

This comment produced laughter from everyone, including Lupin — until I shot him a stern glance.

"I am very happy you all managed to make it here," the man continued, "because the events of the last few days are likely to create some serious problems for all of us. We all know that the police have been snooping about, asking inconvenient questions. And this just might undermine our highly profitable debt collection business. The dead castaway, as that gentleman has now come to be known, has dredged up too much curiosity in town. It's going to become very difficult to do our work with the police nosing around."

"That's right, Salvatore!" someone said.

The man named Salvatore motioned for everyone to be quiet. "I'm not going to waste more time than I need to on words. But the latest news is promising. Apparently Chief Inspector Flebourg won't be calling in reinforcements, and over the next few days, the police plan to scale back their investigation." There was a murmur of approval around the room. "For the benefit of those of you who weren't present at our last meeting, I'll briefly summarize what was discussed. The Parisian — our dead castaway — had run up a rather sizeable gambling debt with us, not even including what he owed the two hotels."

"Have we determined his name yet, Salvatore?" someone asked.

Salvatore threaded his thumbs into his waistcoat and laughed. "What difference does it make what his name was?" he said. "He's dead!" More laughter echoed around the room.

"What about the money he owed us, Macrì?" someone else asked. "If it was the Hotel des Artistes that owed us that much money, I'd empty their cellars and set fire to their curtains. What are we doing about the dead man's debt?"

It took Salvatore Macrì a moment to silence the chaos this comment produced. "Gentlemen, please! Everything has been taken care of!" he said, waving his ringed hands around like a conductor. "The debt has been settled!"

Someone passed Macrì a leather bag, which he opened for everyone to see. It was full of money. Murmurs filled the room. "This is the money our Parisian jeweler friend in Rue du Temple gave me for the diamond necklace that Lady Martigny so kindly donated to our cause!" Macrì said. "We are most grateful to Lady Martigny, but we are particularly grateful for the acrobatic skills of the late Mr. Poussin — or Lambert — who got into her home from the roof and stole the necklace for us. It's such a pity that we didn't find out about his acrobat skills earlier. If he'd worked for us a little longer, we could have easily robbed quite a few rich visitors."

The audience laughed. "But unfortunately," Macrì continued, "his career as a bad gambler and an excellent thief has been cut short."

Salvatore Macrì lifted the bag of money so everyone could see it. "This brings us to the matter of our accounts, which is certainly of great interest to us all. Naturally, I have already taken my commission — a small fee for convincing our two 'friends' in the police department to sabotage the investigations. What remains of the money will be plenty to cover all of the expenses we incurred while entertaining our dead friend with the two names. Almost twelve hundred francs!" His voice rose in a crescendo as Macrì ended his speech.

A series of colorful expressions and curses rapidly spread around the assembly of men. I'd never heard such language before in my life and it served as the final confirmation that these people were the lowest of the low.

By slipping into their meeting, we'd quickly discovered a lot that we hadn't known, and my friends and I were now piecing together all the missing links. That decrepit building was an illegal gambling den, operated by the Italian in the gray suit, Salvatore Macrì. He used it to lighten the wallets of wealthy vacationers looking for entertainment.

Apparently, Macrì also had some shady contacts

with a number of the hotels in the town. Even some of the police were involved. And it seemed that the dead man was so deeply in debt to these violent men that they forced him to steal a lady's jewelry to repay them.

Each piece of the puzzle now seemed to fit into its right place, and everything that had happened until then seemed to make sense. This was why the thugs had ambushed us in the street. It was also why Chief Inspector Flebourg seemed so inept at conducting his investigations — there were officers under him being paid to thwart his every move.

My head was spinning with thoughts of nothing but shady deals and criminals. I'd never dreamed that there were secret organizations at work behind the scene in a pretty little tourist town like Saint-Malo. I'd never imagined there could be such corruption in the police force.

Everyone was milling around Macrì and the bag, pushing and shoving, and yelling things I will not repeat here. I couldn't help but think of pigs around a feeding trough. The meeting was obviously coming to an end, so Sherlock, Lupin, and I tried to move toward the ladder, hoping it would be lowered again soon. I was sweaty and dirty, but it wasn't the dirt on my skin that made me feel so uncomfortable — it was having to be in the same room with these . . . people.

"Wait a minute," Lupin whispered, interrupting my train of thought. He walked off and exchanged a few words with one of the men. Sherlock and I pretended to be deep in conversation, making sure our eyes didn't meet anyone else's.

We heard shouts coming from the lower floor, but at first no one paid attention to them. Then they grew louder and someone began shouting for Salvatore Macrì. The head of the gang listened to the voice for some time — long enough to make the three of us very nervous.

Lupin joined us again and exchanged a glance with Sherlock, the meaning of which I couldn't catch. "This way," said Sherlock, pointing to the door that Macrì had appeared from on the opposite side of the room.

"And we had better be quick about it!" added Lupin.

The three of us scurried as fast as we could across the rotten, old carpets.

The shouts from below became more and more clear: "Salvatore! Salvatore! Someone has gagged Jerome!"

Jerome must have been the guard at the door who Sherlock had knocked out with the pistol. Now there was no doubt that we'd been discovered.

We kept hurrying toward the door. Just as Sherlock was about to grab the handle, the door opened right into his face. Little Spirou was carrying a silver tray full of chipped cups. For an instant, we all stood there staring at each other, not knowing what to do.

Suddenly, Spirou screamed, "Hey! What are you doing here?"

"Out of my way, you idiot!" Sherlock yelled. He pushed Spirou over, the cups and silverware clattering to the ground. We jumped over him and ran for our lives.

Lupin was bringing up the rear. "Don't even try following us!" he yelled, waving the pistol at the astonished faces behind us.

But their shock didn't last more than a few seconds. Roars of anger rose up behind us like a storm tide as we dashed through Salvatore Macrì's apartment.

Chapter 21

MOONLIGHT ACROBATS

Just ahead of me, Sherlock was running for his life. "This way!" he yelled. "Quickly!"

Behind me, Lupin kept looking over his shoulder to check to see if we were being followed. Sherlock bashed open each door with his shoulder and we ran through the rooms, one after another.

"Let us through!" I shouted at two servants. We ran into them, knocking them down.

Lupin pointed the gun at them. "And don't move from there, understand?"

Sherlock bashed open another door and we found

ourselves on a staircase that was as dark as Hades. He grabbed the handrail and peered down. He growled when he saw a man with an ugly face looking straight back at him from farther down the stairs. "They're coming up," Sherlock said. And we could also hear other men catching up to us. That only left us one escape route.

Lupin was the first to run up the stairs. "But if we go up," I started, "how will —"

"Come on! There's no time!" Sherlock yelled, nearly lifting me off my feet as he dragged me along.

We crashed through a rotten wood door and came out on a small terrace on the rooftop. I almost swooned with vertigo. The rooftops of the old quarter stretched out all around us, black and silver in the moonlight, each one nearly leaning against the next. The clouds from that afternoon seemed to have blown away during the night, making the distant sea look like a black mirror. The whole town was bathed in silence, making the angry shouts and footsteps of our pursuers that much more frightening.

"Come on," Lupin said, climbing over the terrace railing.

"What?!" I said. "You can't be serious!" Instead of answering me, Lupin crouched down low on the steep roof and began making his way toward the side of the building. I glanced at Sherlock.

"We have no alternative," he said. "It's frightening, I know. But if the those thugs catch us, I fear they'll give us much more than a scare."

An angry roar from behind us convinced me. I climbed over the railing and began crawling across the tiles. They moved under my weight, creaking ominously. I could see the end of the roof just a few feet away, beyond which was the stinking square we'd crossed earlier that night. I started to wonder how high up we were . . .

I slipped, but Sherlock quickly grabbed me. "Come on, Irene — we're almost there!" he said. It was all the fault of those cursed shoes that were too tight for me. With two kicks, I sent them flying over the edge. I didn't even hear them hit the ground.

The tiles under my bare feet were warm and soft, which calmed me a little. A moment later, we'd joined Lupin on the corner of the roof.

"Hey! You!" shouted someone behind us.

The first of Macrì's henchmen had reached the terrace. A couple of them jumped onto the roof to chase us.

Lupin stood. He glanced at Sherlock and me. "Are you all right?" We both nodded.

Lupin took a deep breath and glanced back at out pursuers, who were now crawling along the roof toward us. He turned back and jumped onto the next building.

"You go next!" Sherlock urged me. Lupin had made it look easy, but as soon as I stood up on the edge of the roof, I felt like the entire world was spinning. "Don't look down, just jump!" shouted Sherlock. He kept turning to keep track of the men, who were getting closer by the second. "Jump, Irene!"

I closed my eyes and opened them, trying to focus on nothing but the roof of the building next door. Then I jumped.

The next thing I knew, I was landing hard on the other roof. I turned and saw Sherlock flying toward me. I got out of his way just in time, and he nimbly rolled onto his back and then to his feet. Then we all started to run.

Lupin moved like a cat. He'd learned from his father how to climb and keep his balance, and didn't seem to be scared of anything. He picked the shortest paths of travel to take and chose the least dangerous places to jump. Thanks to his leadership, we started to get farther away from our pursuers. As we moved, I found that the jumping became easier and more natural. When I heard a shout and a thud behind me, I turned, to see Sherlock struggling back up to his feet. "Don't stop, I'll be fine!" he ordered me. "They're still after us!"

But soon we had lost them, and there were just the three of us wandering among the chimneys and gables of the town. The screams and curses were lost in the night as if they'd never even existed. Lupin guided us to a dark corner between two buildings where we'd be as good as invisible. We rested there for a while, all huddled up together and catching our breath. I realized that my feet were aching miserably, and I was about to say something, but Lupin stopped me. We slowly breathed in the cool night air, trying to calm ourselves down and let the adrenaline wash away.

"I'm going to check to see if the coast is clear,"

Lupin whispered after what seemed an eternity. "Stay here."

I wondered where we were, and tried to get my bearings from the cathedral bell tower. But it was no good. My heart was pounding so hard in my chest that it interrupted my thinking. I saw that I was shivering, too. Sherlock hugged me. I let him, and discovered that he was shivering as well. I can't say how long we stayed there in each other's arms in the shadow of the roof, but eventually I started to feel anxious that Lupin hadn't returned.

I looked up . . . and what I saw petrified me.

"Sherlock?" I whispered. I felt him stir next to me, as if I'd woken him. "Do you see what I see?" A couple of roofs away stood a figure who appeared to be looking straight at us. I felt Sherlock's entire body tense up.

The man was entirely dressed in black. At that distance at night, I couldn't make out his features, but there was no doubt he was facing us.

"Do you think," I whispered in fear, "that he's the Rooftop Thief?"

The man continued to look at us. He remained perfectly still. For a few moments, I thought he might be a statue. When he finally started moving along the edge of the roof, I got chills. I thought again of the hooded figure that I'd seen on the beach. Was he some supernatural being? Why did he keep staring at us? He moved slowly but gracefully over the rooftops as if they were his home.

A sudden idea came to me, which I immediately dismissed — the shadowy figure was too tall and thin to be Mr. Nelson.

"Sherlock, what does he want with us?" I asked.

"Shh!" he answered. We watched the mysterious figure disappear into the darkness. Sherlock started to get up, but a sound on the roof behind us froze him to the spot.

"Sherlock? Irene?" whispered Lupin. "Are you still there? The coast is clear! We can leave now."

I stepped out from the shadows and joined Sherlock. We exchanged a look that implied we shouldn't tell Lupin what we saw."

We scrambled through an open window into a dusty attic, and then followed a steep spiral staircase downstairs. We eventually emerged in an alleyway. It was dark and quiet. The cobblestones felt cold and hard compared to the warmth of the roof tiles.

We checked to our left and right before entering the street.

Without saying a word, we headed toward my home. Every doorway seemed to conceal a new threat. The thugs from the gambling house could have been hiding anywhere. The town felt like a dark trap that was ready to swallow us.

We finally started to relax a little once we passed the statue of René Duguay-Trouin. "What do we do now?" I asked.

"Spirou will talk about us," said Lupin, "but I doubt those men will pay too much attention to him."

"In any case," added Sherlock, "we can always convince him to remain silent."

"Oh yes, Mr. Holmes!" I snapped. "Do you want to behave like those thugs? Solving everything with violence?"

"What else do you suggest?" he answered sharply. "Get your parents to help us?"

"Well, we do need help. These men have no morals and they've already attacked us once," I insisted. "And I doubt it will take them long to figure out who we are."

"I might have an idea," said Lupin. "Remember that I stopped and talked to someone after the meeting in the casino?"

"What about it?" I asked.

"I was trying to find out the name of the policemen who are working for Macrì," Lupin said. "You heard what he said, didn't you? Chief Inspector Flebourg is honest but some of his men aren't."

"Did you find out who they were?" I asked.

"I got two names from him," said Lupin. "If the chief inspector is truly incorruptible, then he will appreciate knowing the names of a couple of dirty cops he has working for him."

"So, what are you going to do?" asked Sherlock.

"Speak to my father," answered Lupin. "And make sure that he passes the information on to Flebourg. After all, we know the name of the leader of this gang. We know he has accomplices all around the town. And we know he stole the necklace."

"No, we don't know that," Sherlock said. "Lambert, Poussin, or whatever his name is, stole the necklace. The Italian only sold it."

"Maybe it's possible to get it back," I said. "We know he sold it to someone in Rue du Temple."

Sherlock waved his hands in the air. "No way!" he cried. Lupin and I looked at him with wide eyes. "Don't you get it? Something doesn't add up about this whole thing! Poussin stole the necklace and therefore repaid his debt. So why was he killed?"

"Maybe they wanted to punish him?" I said.

"For giving them money?" said Sherlock. "I don't think so. If this fellow was such a talented thief, it would have made much more sense for them to continue to use him."

"Yes, Macrì even said that himself," I said.

"Why should we believe anything a villain like Macrì says?!" Lupin argued. "That man would be more than happy to make someone pay for a mistake with his life!"

"Certainly, the man with the two names had a talent for getting himself into trouble," I said.

"That's very true," said Sherlock thoughtfully. "Maybe Macrì wasn't the only villain who had a score to settle with him."

We sat in silence for a while, full of doubts. A dog barked in the distance. "Talk to your father, Lupin," I said. "And let's just keep a low profile for a few days."

So we decided to avoid being seen together in

town or at the harbor until things had calmed down. We parted with one last hug, saying we'd meet again the following Thursday at Ashcroft Manor if nothing else happened . . .

Chapter 22

6 RUE DE MÉZIÈRES

On Monday morning I had no way of knowing if Lupin had spoken to his father about the corrupt police officers, or if Théophraste had passed the information to Chief Inspector Flebourg. Even though the cases seemed as good as solved, my thoughts kept going back to the events of the last couple days.

My father was getting ready to go back to Paris and was giving instructions for preparing a carriage. He was planning to leave right after lunch so he could arrive that evening. The two days he'd spent by the sea seemed to have refreshed him. Even Mother, who was normally so thorny and unfriendly, seemed pleasant.

I went to the post office with Mr. Nelson for two reasons. First, I wanted to see the narrow streets of the town again by daylight so I could try to reconstruct where I'd been the night before. Second, I was too scared to go and do that alone, although I'd never admit that to Lupin or Sherlock.

"Are you feeling all right, Miss Irene?" Horatio asked when we were halfway to the post office. "You haven't said a word."

I was quietly concentrating on every person we saw to see if anyone was looking at me oddly. Maybe Macrì and his men knew who I was, or maybe it was all in my imagination. "I didn't sleep well last night, Horatio," I said.

Horatio stared for a moment at the few clouds scattered in the sky. "You didn't sleep well, or you didn't sleep much?" he asked.

I looked at him, trying to decide if he'd seen me escaping out my window or not. But his face was completely blank. So we traveled the rest of the way to the post office in silence.

There were already quite a few people waiting when we arrived, so we stood patiently in line. Gone was the lively chatter of last Friday. Instead, people were discussing the strange weather. The clouds from the day before seemed to suggest that a storm was on its way.

"Miss!" came a vaguely familiar voice. In an office doorway, I saw the postmaster's friendly face greeting me. I'd spoken to him on Saturday afternoon in the lobby of the Hotel des Artistes.

I returned his greeting, but he beckoned for me to come closer. I asked Mr. Nelson to excuse me and went over.

"I trust you are well, Miss?" the postmaster asked, shaking my hand. "Do you have any letters to send?"

I told him that Mr. Nelson who handled the mail, but I could tell the postmaster didn't really want to talk about that. He walked into his office, went over to his chaotic-looking desk, and started looking for something. "The other day, you piqued my curiosity about a mysterious guest in room thirty-one. Well, apparently your suspicions were incorrect. He never sent any correspondence to the office of any newspaper in Le Havre or Brest."

"So, he wasn't a journalist?" I asked.

"That's the conclusion I came to," the postmaster said.

I thanked him for telling me and said I'd pass the information to my friends. "They won't be very happy, but at least it's something we can rule out," I said.

"But this doesn't mean that there's nothing else interesting about Mr. Lambert!" the postmaster added. "I first discovered that almost all of Lambert's mailings went to just one address in Paris. And then I discovered this!" He pulled out a small, oddly shaped parcel.

"What is it?" I asked.

"A package with no sender listed," he said. "But it's to be sent to the same address in Paris. See here? The sender's part is blank, but the recipient is the same. I found it after comparing the records. The package was already on the Saturday evening coach for Paris, but I brought it back here."

It was a small parcel, too thin to hold jewelry. But while the postmaster was waving it around, I noticed that the address was 6 Rue de Mézières. "So, I told Chief Inspector Flebourg all about it," the postmaster continued, "and he'll be dropping by this morning to pick it up. Perhaps it will be useful in his investigations."

I nodded thoughtfully. Meanwhile, I kept repeating that address in my head. "You might have discovered something very important, sir," I said.

"That's what I've been thinking," he said with a smile. "And I wanted to tell you, since I wouldn't have discovered it if it hadn't been for you and your friends."

I thanked him again and started to leave, but when I was almost at the door a question popped into my head. "Excuse me, sir," I said, turning back toward him, "but if the package was still with the outgoing mail on Saturday, when was it posted?"

"I checked that as well," said the postmaster, "but I can't really give you an answer. The package must have come to the post office last week. Something must have gone wrong, since it remained here longer than it should have."

I decided that it probably wasn't very important, anyway, since I now had an address: 6 Rue de Mézières.

Chapter 23

PARIS

"You should be more pleasant to your mother," my father said as we rode in the carriage to the railway station.

"I know, Papa," I said. "But sometimes it's difficult."

"It's not easy being a good parent, either," Father said. "We're all just trying to do our best."

I wasn't convinced, but had no intention of arguing. My father knew it wasn't fair — the constant ups and downs in my relationship with

Mother were caused by ongoing tension between my parents, which I found out years later when I finally met my real mother. But that summer, when Mr. Nelson loaded Papa's suitcases and my tiny travel bag onto the carriage, I was an adopted child who didn't know she was adopted.

"Goodbye, Horatio!" I cried as the train whistled. "I'll be back home soon!"

"Take care, Miss Adler," he said affectionately. He seemed to want to follow me onto the train as he came within half an inch of giving my hair a friendly ruffle.

Needless to say, it had been easy to convince my father to take me with him to Paris, and almost impossible to convince my mother to let me. The most worrying thing for her was the return train trip, which I'd have to do completely by myself.

"What is the use of going to Paris for just one day?" my mother almost cried.

My excuse was pathetic. I'd said that I needed some books from home and that I couldn't wait for father to send them to me. I'd get them and be back on the train the day after.

"This is a mere whim, Irene! A mere whim!" my mother cried before finally giving in to my stubbornness. She was actually right, for once. But she couldn't even imagine the kind of whim that had actually led me to leave.

I ran to my seat in the carriage and sat down at the window cross from Father. He looked at me with a satisfied little smile, like he was looking at some small, priceless treasure. "There's no stopping you, is there," he said.

With that simple phrase, he made me want to tell him all about my secret adventure.

★ ★ ★

The next day, before dawn, Father left for work. That worked out perfectly, as he didn't know anything about me leaving our home in Saint-Germain-des-Prés and walking to 6 Rue de Mézières. It wasn't far from where we lived.

I crossed Rue Saint-Sulpice and headed toward the gardens before turning onto a side street with low, narrow, and poor-looking apartment buildings. Number 6 was a two-level building that looked quite broken-down.

When I got there, it was before eight in the morning. That gave me about four hours since my train left at noon, and I'd brought everything with me for my return trip, including the books, so I wouldn't have to stop back home before boarding the train.

There was a brass bell attached to the bricks next to the gate. I pulled the cord, producing a delicate tinkle, and then waited. To my surprise, an elderly woman appeared. She was very simply dressed and I got the impression that I must have interrupted her. Her face was very beautiful but her slow movements made her seem much older than she looked.

"May I help you, miss?" she asked, as she dried her hands.

I hadn't been prepared for a conversation so I didn't know how to explain my presence there. So, I chose to be direct.

"I'm sorry to disturb you, madam," I said with a reassuring smile, "but do you know a gentleman by the name of François Poussin? Or possibly Jacques Lambert?"

The woman looked at me, both awed and sad

at the same time. I tried to determine from her expression what was going through her head. "I know that he sometimes sends letters to this address," I continued, still smiling. "So, I was wondering if you, or someone else who lives here, might know him."

The woman suddenly burst into tears. Then she asked me, "What has happened? What has happened to my poor Julien?"

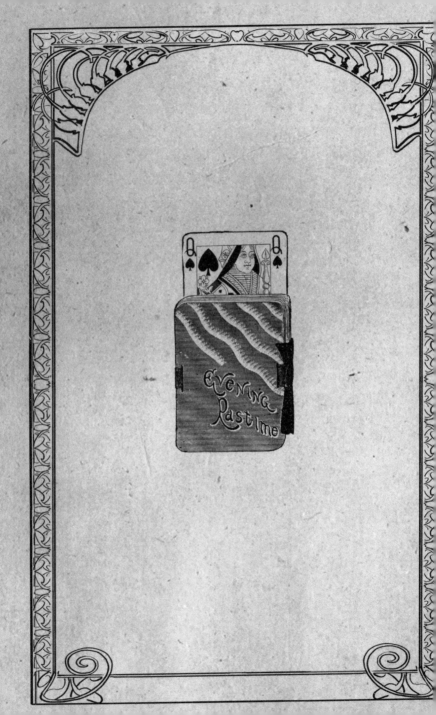

Chapter 24

A MAN WITH MANY NAMES

As planned, on Thursday afternoon, Lupin, Sherlock, and I met at Ashcroft Manor. We all came from different directions and arrived just minutes apart. Sherlock was there before I arrived. Soon after, Lupin arrived in his rowboat.

We all had a lot of news to share. Apparently Chief Inspector Flebourg had been very busy. The tip about the corrupt officers had convinced the honest policeman to call for reinforcements to bring order to the town.

"When they got to the casino," said Lupin, his eyes sparkling, "there wasn't a single sign of Salvatore Macrì."

Lupin explained that the Italian had escaped. However, he'd left his network of contacts exposed, along with all the low-level crooks who were just starting to work for him.

"I don't think it will be long before we also find out who killed the man with two names," Lupin said. He added that the chief inspector had confided in his father that the suicide theory was absolute nonsense — there was a wound on the back of the dead man's head, as if he'd been hit hard. The murderer had then put rocks in his pockets to make him sink, but apparently the body had been dumped in the wrong place because the current brought it back to shore.

"So it must have been one of the low-level gang members," Sherlock said. "Otherwise they wouldn't have made such a stupid mistake."

But we still couldn't make sense of the note we'd found. If it was indeed a murder, the suicide note conflicted that assumption.

As the two boys talked, I stayed quiet. I wanted

to be the last to talk, for dramatic effect, when I told them about the sensational news I'd discovered in Paris.

"I discovered that my mother knows Lady Martigny very well," Sherlock said. "When I found that out, I could have kicked myself. Just think — she's one of three ladies my mother plays bridge with every afternoon!"

Sherlock had learned from his mother that the theft of necklace was a terrible blow for the whole Martigny family. Her husband, who was alerted by telegram about the theft, had even threatened divorce over the matter. The necklace was the most precious of all of the family's heirlooms.

"It does seem, however," said Sherlock, "that my mother's friends are all defending Lady Martigny. The theft was so spectacular and unforeseeable that you can hardly blame her for being careless." He had a distant look on his face, and kept biting his lower lip.

"You think there's more to it?" I asked. "Something we missed?"

"I don't know," Sherlock confessed with a grin,

"but there's one thing that still doesn't make sense to me."

"Do you think there's something false about all of Lady Martigny's friends defending her?" I asked.

"Actually, I think it's quite normal that four friends would support each other when times get tough," Sherlock said. "Although my mother was the last to join the group, the other three — Lady Martigny, Lady Fouchet, and Baroness Gibard — have been vacationing in Saint-Malo for years. What I really don't understand is how it's possible that someone like our man with two names managed to climb down off the roof, steal the necklace, and then go back the way he came without anyone noticing."

"Why is that so amazing?" I asked. I wanted so badly to tell them what I'd discovered in Paris.

"Elementary," Sherlock said. "Do you remember how heavy he was when we turned him over on the beach?" Lupin nodded. "And it wasn't just because of his wet clothes and his pockets full of rocks. He was fat and not at all athletic."

I looked at Lupin, who nodded soberly. "True," he said. "He seemed really out of shape."

Sherlock looked at me as he were waiting for me to add something. But I had nothing to say about the man's physique. I did have something else to say about him, however. "His real name was Julien Lascot." Both of my friends were stunned. "And I know this for certain because I spoke to his mother."

Both Sherlock and Lupin sat down again and stared at me in silence. "His mother was expecting a visit," I said. "She said that she'd always known that one day someone would come knocking on her door to tell her that her son was dead. But she'd always imagined it would be a policeman, not a girl like me." I smiled, remembering the woman inviting me to make myself comfortable in her simple but well-maintained sitting room.

"The Lascots have never been wealthy," I continued. "Julien's father was a bricklayer and his business had a good reputation with his customers, but apparently he didn't want Julien to study or to follow in his footsteps. So Julien ran away from home ate the age of sixteen and never returned. Although his mother didn't tell me as much, I realized that Julien became a rogue who lived by his wits and was obsessed with the idea of proving to the world how good he was. He wrote home once in a while to tell his parents about his adventures and to brag about his successes. According to his mother, though, her son was just wasting his money, his good looks, and charm on his vices: gambling and adultery!"

I waited a moment for my last sentence to sink in before I continued. "Julien was an accomplished liar. He'd probably never told the truth in his entire life. Every time a deal or a bet went wrong, he'd move on to another city and start all over again. This was why his mother had always expected that one day his crimes would catch up with him."

"But are you sure that this Julien was the man we found on the beach?" Lupin asked.

I told them about my meeting with the postmaster and how the police will probably eventually come to the same conclusion. "I asked Mrs. Lascot not to tell anyone about my visit," I added. "And she promised that she'd keep my secret. 'I'd always expected it,' she said as I was leaving. 'It hurts to say it about your own child, but bad follows bad.' Then she said goodbye."

Sherlock, Lupin, and I talked for a long time

about everything I'd discovered. It was Lupin who eventually tied up all the loose threads. "Bad follows bad," he began, repeating Mrs. Lascot's bitter words. "This explains everything. Like Sherlock said, the dead man wasn't a professional thief, just a person who lived a life of lies, scams, and the occasional theft. He got mixed up with people like Macrì, and maybe people even worse than him. By doing that, he signed his own death warrant."

Our investigations into the case of the dead castaway, as it had come to be known in Saint-Malo, were now more or less over. There were certainly still important things to be discovered, like whether it was Macrì or some other thug who ordered the murder of Lascot. But now that we knew what kind of man the dead castaway was, it seemed obvious that his death was the result of getting in over his head with the criminal underworld.

All three of us were proud of everything we'd discovered during our investigations. We were filled with excitement, and spent hours telling each other again and again about all the bizarre and dangerous things that had happened over the last week.

I watched the waves breaking lazily before us, slowly growing with the rising tide. In less than an hour, we'd need to row back to the harbor. "Julien Lascot had it coming to him," I said out of the blue. "The only real victim in it all was Lady Martigny."

"I wouldn't say she was the only victim," Lupin said from behind me. He was shuffling some cards, trying a trick that his father had shown him.

"What do you mean?" I asked.

Lupin quickly counted the cards on the sand in front of him and said, "That's why it's not working: one card is missing." He'd organized them into suits and found that the missing card was the Queen of Spades.

"That was the same card that Julien Lascot was using as a bookmark in the little red book we found in the hotel room!" I said.

Sherlock turned as pale as a ghost. He stared at the cards without speaking. It scared me.

"Sherlock?" I asked, trying to shake off the fear. "Sherlock, what's wrong?"

"This isn't possible. This just isn't possible," he said to himself. "It simply is not possible."

"What isn't possible?" I asked. I noticed he was staring at the cards. "Whose cards are those?"

"They're my mother's," Sherlock answered. He said it so quietly that I hardly heard him.

Chapter 25

THREE LADIES

That Friday I convinced Mr. Nelson to help us. He was to create some diversion to make Sherlock's mother late to her card game so we had some time to talk to the other players before she arrived.

We knocked on Lady Martigny's door and had her servant announce us as "Mrs. Holmes's children, looking for their mother." We strolled casually into the sitting room, which, according to the lady of the house, was next door to the room from where Julien Lascot had stolen the necklace.

"Master Holmes," said Lady Martigny, recognizing him. But her courteous reception wavered slightly when she saw two strangers in the place of Mycroft and Violet, Sherlock's brother and sister. However, she was too polite to ask what was going on.

"I'm afraid that your mother has not yet arrived," said Lady Martigny, obviously wondering why all these strange children had invaded her sitting room.

Sherlock gave a slight bow. "I am aware of that, Lady Martigny," he replied. "Lady Fouchet, Baroness Gibard — I apologize for the interruption."

"Well, we haven't quite started our game yet, Master Holmes," said Lady Martigny. "As I say, we are still waiting for your mother to arrive."

"I fear, however, that some interruption is unavoidable," said Sherlock. "But first I would like to introduce my friends, Miss Adler and Master Lupin."

"Adler?" clucked Baroness Gibard. "By chance are you the daughter of Mr. Leopold Adler?"

"At your service, Baroness Gibard," I said.

"We had a very pleasant Sunday afternoon tea," the baroness told me.

I looked around. The three ladies glowed like gold. They were all wearing beautiful jewelry and elegant formal clothes. The room was bright ochre yellow and was hung with tapestries and paintings with gilded frames. On the center table was a beautiful arrangement of lilies. Crystal trays were piled with cakes, soon to be joined by teacups and a teapot.

"I am afraid, however, that I am not aware of your family, Master Lupin," Lady Martigny said with a certain arrogance in her voice.

"I would imagine that you would be aware of the family of my mother, Henriette d'Andresy, and my cousins, the Dreux-Soubises," Lupin said flatly.

Lady Fouchet brought her hand to her mouth. "Good heavens! Most certainly I am. Oh, you poor child!"

Lupin raised an eyebrow and smiled a smile that could have cut through the thick brocade curtains. "Yes," he said, "I am the son of the famous gymnast who brought ruin upon the d'Andresy family."

Lady Fouchet blushed the color of a tomato. "Forgive me, my dear boy. I absolutely did not want to imply any such thing."

"Excuse me," Sherlock interrupted, "but I fear that this discussion is not leading us anywhere. And since time is short, I would like to say that the three of us have given much thought to coming here today to tell you what we have to say. And that we have collected overwhelming evidence to support it all."

"Overwhelming evidence, Master Holmes?" repeated Lady Martigny.

"Exactly, Lady Martigny," Sherlock said. "And I imagine that you know perfectly well what I'm talking about." I noticed the two ladies seated at the table exchange glances, and Lady Fouchet's lip started twitching. I decided it was already obvious which of the three ladies would give in first to Sherlock's questions.

"Master Holmes," Lady Martigny replied, "I am afraid that your words and behavior seem rather inappropriate."

"As are yours, if I may be so bold," said Sherlock. "And I would now ask you to let me speak, because I can assure you that this situation is just as embarrassing for me as it is for you." I heard Sherlock's voice shaking from nervousness and realized he was struggling to control himself.

Lupin stopped Lady Martigny from picking up the bell to call her servants, and politely asked her to sit down.

"We know what happened with Julien Lascot,"

began Sherlock. "Or perhaps I should use the name you knew him by: François Poussin, or perhaps Jacques Lambert." All three ladies looked visibly shaken. "So, would you prefer to tell us what happened or would you like us to do it for you?"

"I don't know what you are alluding to, Master Holmes," said Lady Martigny, quickly recovering her faculties. "I can't even begin to imagine the impudence that has led you to my house with —"

"It was me!" Baroness Gibard cried out.

"Annette!" snapped Lady Martigny.

"I confess!" the Baroness continued. "There's no point trying to keep it a secret any longer! If these children were able to figure it out, how long do you think it will take the police? I cannot live with this guilt! Every night when I dream, I see him!"

"He's dead, Annette!" screamed Lady Martigny. "He's dead!"

"Yes, yes, he's dead! You're right!" she replied. "And I killed him!"

"It wasn't you who killed him!" cried Lady Martigny. "It wasn't your fault!"

"She's right, Annette," said Lady Fouchet, who then turned to me and smiled weakly with embarrassment. "It wasn't any one of us who killed him. We all did it." She slowly got up from the table and dropped a deck of cards down on the green cloth. "That's right, my dear children: three killers in one sitting room!"

I was shocked. Lupin was, too, by the looks of it. Sherlock, however, seemed not the least bit surprised.

Lady Martigny then explained that Julien Lascot had introduced himself to her and Lady Fouchet under different names, not knowing that the two were best friends. Lascot's technique was the same with both: a nice smile, a few polite compliments, flowers, pleasant conversation, and the odd reference to the right people and places in Paris. It was all a ruse to create the impression that he was a rich gentleman in order to get himself admitted into the homes of each of the two ladies.

Once Lascot was there, he helped himself to their jewels. So Lady Martigny's necklace wasn't stolen by an acrobatic thief who'd climbed into her house from the roof, like she'd told the police, but simply by a guest.

Surprisingly, she'd discovered the theft long before she told the police. By the time Lascot was found dead, the necklace had been gone for more than ten days. Lady Martigny had been trying to find some way of letting her husband know about the theft without admitting to being naive enough to have let a perfect stranger into their house.

Lady Fouchet had also been one of Lascot's victims, but her losses had only included a couple of pieces of silverware and some pearl earrings. But when she spoke to Lady Martigny about it, the two quickly figured out that it had been the same man who had tricked and robbed them both. And when they told the third lady, a longtime friend of theirs, they discovered that Lascot had also just had himself introduced to her. Baroness Gibard was exactly the type of woman Lascot preyed on: a fashionable, older lady who was very rich.

So the three had set a trap for him at a dinner at the home of the baroness. The man had presented himself at her door dressed in fine clothes, including a shirt with a turndown collar, a jacket, cuff links, and a suit — the same clothes he'd been wearing when he was found dead on the beach the day after. Lascot didn't suspect a thing. He was relaxed, even bold. Thanks to the necklace he'd stolen, he'd paid off his debt to Salvatore Macrì and thought he didn't have a care in the world. What he hadn't considered was that secrets don't stay secrets for long in small resort towns like Saint-Malo where people know more than they pretend.

Once inside the house, Lascot immediately saw that he'd stumbled into a difficult situation. He was confronted by all three of the ladies. They accused him of theft. He responded by rejecting their accusations. An argument followed. And then there was a scuffle. Baroness Gibard pushed him, and Mr. Lascot stumbled on the edge of a rug. He fell, hitting his head violently on the corner of a table. He died instantly.

Naturally, the first reaction of two of the ladies was to call the authorities. But Lady Martigny thought otherwise. Since dead men tell no tales, making the accidental death of the thief look like something else would give her the perfect story for hiding the true circumstances of the theft of the necklace from her husband. Both her friends knew that Mr. Martigny would never forgive his wife for letting a stranger enter their home, so they agreed to help her with her plan.

Baroness Gibard's home directly overlooked the sea, and the family kept a small boat moored at the private jetty. The three ladies dragged Lascot's body to the boat, filled his pockets with rocks, and took him out to sea. So that people would think it was suicide, they put a forged suicide note in his pocket. The police, of course, never found it. But since the women were very inexperienced with the sea, they threw the body overboard at a point where the tide took it straight back to shore. As a result, when the body was found, Lady Martigny still hadn't reported the acrobatic theft of the family jewels to the police.

But otherwise, the plan had worked perfectly. That is, until we arrived in their sitting room.

"So what do you intend to do?" Lady Martigny asked Sherlock once the whole story had been told. "Will you tell the police?"

The question lingered for a long time in the sickly sweet air. These three naive ladies had accidentally killed a man and then tried to hide the body. What they ended up doing, partly because of us, was help Chief Inspector Flebourg uncover an entire criminal network. A network that even had members of the local police working for it. This has led to the capture of numerous criminals, although not the people who were behind Lascot's death.

"What do we intend to do?" answered Sherlock. "Just one thing: discover the whole truth, right down to the smallest details that still need to be explained." Without a word, he disappeared into the hallway.

A moment later, a dark shape emerged from the shadows of the hallway. I screamed, startling Lady Martigny and her guests, and I grabbed Lupin by the arm. It was the hooded man I'd seen on the beach! What was he doing there? Who was he?

The answers came quickly. From under the blue hood came a laugh and, a moment later, the face of Sherlock Holmes.

"Sherlock, you're a fool!" I exclaimed angrily.

"Sorry if I don't share your opinion, my dear Irene," he answered. "You might like to know that I've just solved the mystery of the man in the blue cloak. Or, more accurately . . . Baroness Gibard!" With a dramatic gesture, he revealed the coat of arms of the noble woman's family stitched into the hood.

The baroness looked like she was about to faint. "Oh, I — I do not," she stammered.

"Calm down, Baroness," Lupin said soothingly.

"After what we did, I was frantic," the baroness said. "I could not sleep at night, and during the day I constantly paced up and down the beach, hidden beneath that dark cloak. I kept looking out to sea, convinced that at any moment I would see François' body. And then suddenly my nightmare came true. On the beach, I saw him! I saw him there!" The baroness began sobbing, unable to continue her story. But at least the mystery of the hooded figure had been cleared up.

But Lady Martigny's question still hung in the air like an ominous echo: "So what do you intend to do?"

As if on cue, a breathless Mrs. Holmes burst into the room. She apologized for being delayed, blaming her talkative butler. But then she saw that Sherlock was there. "William? What are you doing here?"

Lupin and I took a step back, smiling shyly. Sherlock pulled the deck of cards with the missing Queen of Spades out from his pocket. With a forced smile, he said, "We came to bring you these, Mama. You must have dropped them."

And then we left.

Chapter 26

THE FINAL MYSTERY

We decided to send a letter to the chief inspector, being very careful that he wouldn't be able deduce who wrote it. But in the days that followed, nothing seemed to happen. The case of the dead castaway had seemingly been forgotten about. People also stopped talking about the theft of Lady Martigny's diamond necklace.

In the weeks after our investigation, the little group of bridge players broke up and Mrs. Holmes had to find new friends with whom to pass the long summer afternoons. The three noblewomen stopped being seen around town, but if that was because they'd been arrested, we never found out.

As for me and our little group, we'd achieved what we'd set out to do: discover the truth. As for how this truth was used, or who it served, we really didn't care — not that we could have done anything about that, anyway. Sherlock, Lupin, and I continued to see each other and continued with our training. Théophraste was an excellent teacher, but he also had a dark side that sometimes made me uneasy. I preferred it when there were just the three of us, punching the bag or trying different martial arts techniques.

Sometimes we'd read the classics we loved the most out loud, performing them in front of Ashcroft Manor. Other times, we would individually perform different sleight-of-hand tricks while the other two tried to discover how they worked.

We also went fishing with Sherlock's older brother, who proved to be far nicer than Sherlock had led us to believe. I also met his sister, Violet, and gave her one of my smallest dresses. Our parents never met, and we worked hard to make sure they wouldn't, for they could have ruined everything in that way that only adults know how to do.

But there still remained one small, unresolved detail of our first adventure together: the mystery of the Rooftop Thief. The whole thing had worried Lupin terribly, since the man's incredible acrobatic skills had made him suspect that it was his own father. It wasn't until many years later that Lupin finally found out the truth about his father: he had never been the Rooftop Thief.

★ ★ ★

On the night of the next full moon, Sherlock called to me from the street. I joined him immediately via the "Lupin shortcut" — that is, my bedroom window. He led me through the old streets of the town to a house, where he picked the lock to open the door. We followed the stairs up to the roof. He was almost completely silent, only mumbling in response to my questions.

When we were up on the roof, he sat down, apparently waiting for something. I soon found out what it was. With the rest of the town asleep, we watched as a thin, black silhouette of a man moved slowly across the roof opposite of us. The Rooftop Thief was just a stone's throw away. He seemed to be both looking at us and ignoring us at the same time.

This time, however, he was close enough for me to recognize him. "Dr. Morgoeuil?" I said in disbelief. "But what's he doing?"

Sitting beside me, Sherlock was wearing a sneer that I eventually came to loathe. He wore it every time he'd discovered something before anyone else had. "He's sleepwalking," he explained. "Whenever there's a full moon, he comes out to walk on the roofs." Dr. Morgoeuil was unmarried and had lived alone for over fifty years.

That was the simple story behind the legendary Rooftop Thief. With that revelation, we felt like we'd finally solved all of the mysteries of Saint-Malo. Although we still didn't really know anything about ourselves.

But there was still plenty of time for that.

IRENE ADLER

SHERLOCK
LUPIN & ME

KEEP YOUR
EYES
PEELED
FOR THE
NEXT BOOK
IN THE
SHERLOCK,
LUPIN & ME
SERIES!

Capstonepub.com

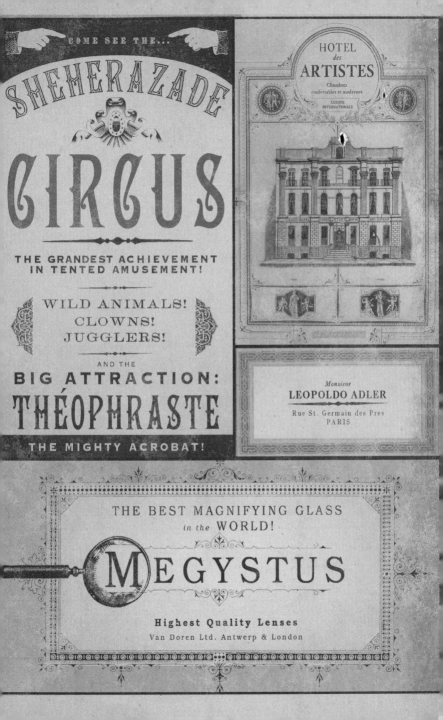

NAVIGATION AÉRIENNE

LOUIS C.E. GODARD
34, Rue Lacroix, 34
BATIGNOLLES-PARIS

AÉRONAUTE
Au Grand Ballon captif de Paris, 1878-1879
de Nice, 1881 de Turin, 1884

Prof.^r À L'ÉCOLE AÉROSTATIQUE MILITAIRE ITALIENNE

EXPÉRIENCES & ASCENSIONS
SCIENTIFIQUES

ÉTUDE & CONSTRUCTION D'AÉROSTATS
en tous genres
POUR INVENTEURS & AÉRONAUTES

BALLON CAPTIF A VAPEUR
& Appareils à gaz, roulant
POUR LES ARMÉES EN CAMPAGNE

DESCENTE EN PARACHUTE

VÉLOCE AÉRIEN
BREVETÉ

GRANDS ATELIERS SPÉCIAUX
de Construction Aérostatique & d'Expérience
23, Rue de la Fédération (Champ de Mars)
BUREAUX & CORRESPONDANCE
Rue Vintimille, PARIS

MAIRIE de NANTES
1 AOUT 87
Bureau du ...
N° ...

Paris, le   188

Monsieur le Maire,

J'ai l'honneur de solliciter de votre bienveillance
la faveur de participer à l'éclat des Fêtes de votre
ville.

Je suis muni d'un matériel aérostatique complet
construit dans mes ateliers et comprenant des Ballons
depuis 300 mètres jusqu'à 2800 mètres cubes, pouvant
enlever de une à dix personnes

Je me charge de tout genre d'ascension scienti-
fique et avec voyageurs, d'ascension double entre deux
ballons, de descente en parachute, &c, &c

Dans l'espoir, Monsieur, que vous voudrez
bien me comprendre dans le Programme de vos Fêtes

Je vous prie d'agréer l'expression de mes
sentiments distingués

Louis Godard

DONA-CEYLON
FINEST BREAKFAST TEA MIXTURE

DONA-CEYLON
ESTABLISHED IN EDINBURGH SINCE 1869

A UNIQUE INVIGORATING BLEND
of HEARTY BLACK CEYLON TEAS

ESTABLISHED IN EDINBURGH SINCE 1869

LEBLANC CADENAS ANTIVOL

LEBLANC CADENAS ANTIVOL

EN ACIER
INDESTRUCTIBLE
INVIOLABLE!

Aciéries M. Leblanc - ROUEN

LE TERREUR DE TOUS VOLEURS!

1900   1880

FANNY GODARD

H. POTTIER
PROF.^r ...
Maison Julienne
ST MALO

THE
DARK LADY
THE WORLD-FAMOUS PRESTIGIOUS BRAND

54 QUALITY CARDS' DECK

GENTLEMEN'S CAPS and HATS
1805   1868
MCARDLE & WILLIAMSON

EXQUISITELY TAILORED FROM THE BEST HIGHLANDS' WOLLENS